WASTING AWAY

WASTING AWAY

To Val
May you always shine
in all you do.
Theo.
11. 16. 2015.

a novel

THEODORA O. AGYEMAN-ANANE

www.theodoraofosuhima.com

First Edition

Printed and bound in the United States of America

First Love – Fiction // Bully – Fiction // Verona (Italy) – Fiction // Anorexia – Fiction // Self-esteem – Fiction // Psychological fiction// Ghana (West-Africa) // Teen pregnancy – Fiction // Parents and offspring //

ISBN-10:1516866428
ISBN-13:9781516866427

For Andrew.
Good things come to those who wait.

PROLOGUE
Verona, Italy, March 2000

Susanna chooses a pair of faded jeans and hurries inside the fitting room, securing the lock behind her. She double checks; safely closed. Her shaking fingers unzip her loose jeans. She feels lighter, free of all the dark feelings of winter. She can hear Aunt Marta's snotty voice, as if she were in the fitting room with her. *Cara, pastel colours enhance your olive skin.* A few months ago, Susanna would have disregarded her aunt's comment. Aunt Marta – full of herself, believing that being a models' agent allowed her to criticize people's fashion sense. But now, Susanna *wants* Marta's opinions. Because of Brad. She leans against the fitting room wall and closes her eyes. All because of Brad. His honey-coloured eyes. Those soft lips, they take her breath away. He'll be her boyfriend again once she looks like a model.

Susanna gazes at her image in the mirror. Her curls bounce loose on her shoulders. Last year Brad told her she looked good with her hair down but today it's impossible to tame. She strips off her clothes and turns right and left couple of times. She should be proud. The mirror reflects a lean body thanks to her recent food choices. The dark skin beneath her eyes is the badge of her new eating plan; less carbohydrate, more lean meat and lots of water. She is sleeping less and exercising more. She rises onto the balls of her feet to give herself a little height. Turns, looks over her shoulder at her bottom and the sight whooshes the good feeling right out of her. Every time she looks at her huge backside, she sees a big mandolin. With shaking fingers she slides back into the jeans.

7

"How're you getting on," the shop assistant calls from outside the fitting room. Chiara, her name tag reads. Susanna, yanks her top down over her hips to hide her bottom, steps out of the change room.

"*Mamma mia,*" Chiara flaps her fingers in the air. "*Sei magnifica.* Why were you wearing those loose jeans?"

Susanna just says coolly, "I'll take this pair and another in white." They walk together to the till. Chiara's wavy blonde hair shifts on her shoulders. Her small butt tight in a pair of *Diesels.*

"Good choice. I wish I could fit into them. Look at my butt," Chiara looks away from the digits on the till, "I'm not kidding, you could be a model, you know?"

A model, Susanna thinks. How could she become a model? The last time she checked the model catalogue at the agency, a model has to be at least five foot seven. Shop assistants are never honest. She may look good in these jeans but there is a big difference between looking good and modelling. Susanna takes the shopping bags from Chiara without smiling.

Outside, the scent of cherry and peach blossoms mingles with the aroma of freshly baked bread from the bakery across the street. At the bus stop, her belly thunders. She looks at the bakery. Like a zombie drawn by human smell she retraces her steps and peers through the glass window. Her eyes fall on a group of girls snuggled up at a table, drinking sweet frothy cappuccino and biting into sugar-glazed doughnuts, their lips shiny and sparkling. Susanna smiles proudly. How much stronger she is getting each passing day! Resisting unhealthy eating habits! Since December she has cut out sugar, salt and fast food. She looks again at the girls. Wets her lips. The way they touch each other's shoulders and giggle when they turn to a group of boys sitting on the other side of the bakery makes Susanna feel the urge to enter the shop.

"How can I help you today?" The server with chubby rosy cheeks smiles and asks Susanna as soon as she enters.

"Hmm... I'm just looking." Susanna tucks her hair behind an ear, looks around and bites off the skin of her thumb nail. In front of her, like a rainbow, are assorted colours of macaroons. Fruit tartlet with a crispy, buttery pastry crust, filled with crème and topped with strawberries. Chocolate ganache truffles coated in cocoa powder. Sponge cake topped with airy mousseline cream, fresh strawberries, and a thin layer of marzipan, mini croissants and doughnuts.

"They're delicious." the server points at the ocean of sorted pâtissières with sparkling eyes "These macaroons here, the ones with raspberry filling coated in chocolate, are our speciality. They're made of two pure almond shells filled with jam."

Susanna wants to resist, tries to resist: "Okay then." she says "Can I have three, please?" She wants to kick herself in her enormous butt, but it's too late. She hurries out from the bakery with the macaroons clutched in a small brown bag.

The wind tosses dust around, watering her eyes. Most of the pedestrians are wearing short sleeves, but Susanna clasps her sweater tightly at the neck. She walks back to take bus 85, then instead of waiting for it, she hurries past the *edicola* near Verona Arena and walks into the small park in piazza Bra. She sits on an empty bench and takes one macaroon from its wrapping; smooth in her hand. She closes her eyes, inhales the caramel smell of the sugar. Opens her mouth, but Brad's voice, as if in a dream, echoes *"...like a model... like a model."* She loses her appetite.

Susanna squeezes the macaroon. The dust of the meringue falls out of her palm, leaving behind the moist raspberry filling and chocolate coating. Pigeons fly to peck at the offering. Watching the greedy birds dance ravenously, pecking, squawking for more, Susanna feels stronger and stronger.

The images of herself and Brad in the wooden hut, last December, reel on her mind. These are followed by the scene at the youth chalet, when she meets Brad's friends for the first time. She tries to block the words Volpe said to her on that cold December night. For a few minutes, she manages. She turns her attention to the fountain shimmering in the spring sun. Next to it are two German students posing and sticking their tongues out for pictures. The guide is shouting how the Arena was built in the first century AD behind the city walls. Then he points at the bronze statue of Victor Emmanuel II, the first king of Italy, atop a horse and says loudly in his microphone "It was inaugurated on January 9th 1883, five years to the day after his death."

Susanna shifts her attention to some people hurrying up from the bench in front of her, probably off to shop or work in the many designer boutiques along busy Via Mazzini. Just ahead of them she sees some girls from the recruiting catalogue she stole from her aunt's modelling agency. Their skinny legs, wrapped in jeans as tight as if it's their second skin. Watching them makes her realize how badly she needs to lose more weight. Chiara, the shop assistant, was lying. You can't become a model with Susanna's thunder thighs.

The pigeons are dancing, wanting more meringue dust. Susanna takes a bite. One bite won't make her fat. But the sticky sugary taste on her lips feels like overcooked bacon fat. It reminds her of her greedy old self. She spits it out, pushes the thoughts back and returns to catch bus 85.

She passes the *edicola* and the owner, an old man over sixty, shouts *"Ciao, bella moretta."* Susanna's heart jumps into her throat. One thing she hates is to be called beautiful blackie. *Pervert.* Susanna grimaces at him.

Once on the bus, she sits close to the window. To avoid anyone sitting next to her she places her shopping bag on the free seat. At each stop she counts how many people get off and on the bus. So far thirty people have gotten on and about fifteen have gotten off. When the bus passes another newsagent she decides to go buy the new issue *Cioè*. She stands up to ring the bell just as the bus driver whams the brake. A guy on a scooter tumbles by. Susanna can't grab the bar in time. Everything rushes like a meteorite.

She wants to pretend nothing has happened but the force pulling her down is stronger than her will. She lies there, powerless, for what seems an eternity. Voices – the bus driver asking, "Are you okay? Are you okay?" A child crying in the distance; or maybe it's her. Images of Brad's honey eyes and dimples are the things that stick.

She wakes up hours later in a hospital bed. Her mother's orange flower scent is the first thing that brings her to reality. Susanna opens her eyes, squints at the bright light pouring onto the white walls. Looking out the window, brown wavy hair pulled into a tight ponytail, is her mother. The way the light filters through makes her already small waistline thinner. She is wearing a cream cardigan over a pair of denims, her rich but not too flashy uniform.

Susanna throws the cover off her legs, trying to sit up. But tubes snake from her arms. She gasps. Her mother turns to her.

"Oh, *amore!* Be careful." Olga comes quickly, runs her fingers through her daughter's curls. Susanna looks at her mother's face. Today she wears a light makeup. Forty-five years old without wrinkles, thanks to facial massages and the occasional Botox. Sadness veils her eyes like the grey before a downpour. Susanna closes her eyes. Olga kisses her daughter's forehead.

"I'm fine." Susanna snaps. She pushes her head into the bleached hospital pillow then wets her chapped lips and sighs. Having her mother there makes her feel like rinsing herself under a shower of sand. She loathes herself for causing such a fuss. She hates the bus driver for braking like a lunatic. She despises whoever called an ambulance. Above all, she hates herself for not keeping her balance. Her headache climbs to full force. She fights back the image of Brad's beautiful eyes.

"The doctor said you fainted because you've been starving yourself." Her mother's words are metal nails on her ears. Susanna turns away to watch the birds outside her room, dancing over the trees in blossom. Everything changed when Brad sat next to her that September morning.

CHAPTER 1
Verona, Italy, September 1999

Having Brad as a classmate was a dream come true. His was the number every girl was dying to have. That year he enrolled in my French class because, as someone told me later on, he wanted to impress a Parisian girl he'd met at summer camp. The first day he walked into class, a whirlpool of emotions, made of nervousness and happiness, pulled me under my desk. I was on cloud nine when he sat in the seat next to mine. Though Professore Cazzanella, who we call Prof. Cazzanella for short, was still calling our names, Brad turned to introduce himself. He smiled boldly, with his eyes half-closed. Though I'd seen him around school before, I looked up at him as if it was the first time I'd set eyes on his handsome face. I swear, I had never seen such intoxicating dimples as his. He had one of those faces that could have come straight from a Calvin Klein catalogue. High cheek bones, fine nose made perfect by the tiniest scar on the bridge; dark brown hair cut short and sexy; honey coloured eyes and a mouth stained dark peach with a full bottom lip. He dressed like a runway model. That particular morning, he was wearing a pair of tight, faded denim jeans and a chequered blue shirt.

"Susanna." I introduced myself, but then thought, *avoid his eyes, and look at the notebook.* Awkward silence, which seemed to last forever followed, until I finally broke it. "I know you. You're on the hockey team, right?"

"How do you know?" He slowly applied balm on his lips. I couldn't take my eyes off them.

"Everyone at Liceo knows who you are." French was one of my favourite subjects, but that morning I couldn't have cared less. I tried to return my attention to the lesson but I couldn't concentrate on the phrase Prof. Cazzanella was explaining. Brad's smile had overtaken my universe. In all my days at Liceo Dante, nothing had disturbed me so much as the presence of Brad in the first hour of my third year in high school.

I turned onto my left and my eyes met with Melanie's, who is known as "the witch" due to her love for everything purple and black, from lip-gloss to clothes. I quickly look back at the pages in front of me *Natalie's not going to believe it when I tell her about Brad giving me attention.* I trembled as I thought of telling Natalie my secret. I couldn't wait to see my best friend, who studied art at a different high school few blocks away. Unfortunately, I would have to delay my story until after an awful hour of gym.

Gym classes were my nightmare. The *professoressa* made us do exercises that were so embarrassing. Most of the stretching exercises consisted of lying on the floor with our legs in the air. Often my t-shirt would peel off my back, revealing my dark skin. The guys would sing in chorus, "Susanna, bare-backed porno star." These episodes made me uncomfortable because I've always thought porn stars were stupid and uneducated. Just remembering those words felt like my face had been slapped. And some of the other guys called me *mandolino*. One day Fenice, a chubby cheeks, freckled face guy, told me that those same guys thought I had a big, round bottom that protruded like a mandolin. I took the comment badly and from that day on, I'd started hiding my bottom under oversized tops. I wanted a bottom as flat as a surfboard, but I hadn't got around to doing anything to achieve my dream-dierriere.

For gym that first morning, I wore a pair of knee-length shorts, a long undershirt tucked into them and a large t-shirt over it all.

When I went downstairs to go to gym class, I found Carla Scaffoldin, one of the girls from German class, sitting on a bench near the parking lot with her new Ericsson mobile phone up to her ear and a cigarette in the other hand. I'd known her since we were in grade three, but we'd never gotten on very well. In my opinion she was a little stuck-up and, though just a few months older than me, she pretended to know a lot about sex. The guys at school liked her because they thought she was beautiful and always ready to have a laugh. In fact, her secret nickname was Carla *la* troia.

One of her favourite pastimes was putting on make-up during lessons. The teachers didn't really like her either, especially when she came into class wearing a mini skirt or dress that was just too short. I remember one day while Prof. Bergamini, the professor of religion, was explaining the differences between the various religions, Carla started to put on her bronzer. Bergamini suspended her for two days, but Carla took the suspension as a free holiday. She didn't care whether her grades were being affected or not. I'm sure she would have cared if her suspension was going to bother her father, who was divorced from her mother. She tried in any way to get his attention but she felt he wasn't there enough for her, especially since he started dating his new girlfriend.

While she was suspended I met her at a party and in one of her drunken moments she confided in me. "My mother is right, my father doesn't care about our broken family. She's right to hate him. Why she married him is beyond me. I'm never going to marry a man like that." Carla's pretty face twisted with anger as she spewed out her venom. "You know he lives with that bitch? Anna, fucking bitch! I hate her. I hate her so much. She's ruined our family. Before her, my father was always there for my brother and me."

I felt so sorry to see her in that state. But, when Carla was not in an emotional state of mind, nobody could help but dislike her a little. She knew how to attract attention to her perfect body and she flaunted it. On that first day of term, as a group of us were standing in the courtyard, she was wearing a tankini top with an open cardigan. My eyes fell on her flat tummy and long, toned legs. Her shorts were far too short and tight for gym. I knew that when she dressed like that she didn't have any intention of joining us in the workouts. She wanted to turn on the guys and torture the girls with envy.

"Ciao, ciao." she said, rolling her eyes up. She punched the keypad of her phone, threw the remains of the cigarette to the ground and stomped heavily on it. "Errrr, I can't stand him. He is such a pain." She rolled her eyes at me again.

"Who?" I asked, confused.

"Luca, my ex-boyfriend. Who else?" she looked at me as if I should know who she was talking about.

"Ah." I pretended to care.

"He cheats on me, then he pretends we're back together. I don't have time to waste with losers like him." She puffed her lips and applied more lip gloss, then looked at me as if I was staring too much.

"Going to gym today?" I asked, just to fill the awkward silence that followed.

"Are you crazy? Do I need it?" She did a perfect little pirouette. I looked her up and down. Five foot six, slim, with curves in all the right places; naturally curling, light blond hair and gorgeous, milky skin. Did she need to work out on our school's grimy gym floor like the rest of us? I didn't think so.

"Guess who's in my class?" I quickly changed topic.

"Brad? I know. Remember? He's Giulio's friend." Carla's eyes lit up at the last name. Giulio was another popular guy in school; not as perfectly cute as Brad, but he was the captain of the hockey team and he was always surrounded by cheerleaders. Recently, Carla seemed to have him under her spell. I guess she was intrigued by the age difference. Giulio was eighteen years old, two years older than us and doing his final year. I looked down at the gravel in the courtyard to avoid Carla reading my thought about when she and Giulio are together.

"Susanna, Susanna, Miss naked back *porno star*!" It was the grouchy voice of Andrea, a guy from the Spanish class, with his big ugly mouth and acne-infected nose. He always took great pleasure in tormenting me.

"Hey, Andrea, drop it." Brad was suddenly at my side and intervening in my defence. *Dio Mio, how sweet is he?* I never knew a school mate could be so nice. My mind was having its own private party about Brad.

"*Ragazzii!* Hurry up!" the professor shouted from the gym entrance. "Don't waste my time with your laziness." She looked relaxed and tanned. Usually, she snapped at us when we were tardy, but not that morning. In fact, it looked as if she was in the mood to joke with us. "At the pace you're all moving, a turtle would win the race."

Carla whispered in my ear. "Do you know she met her new guy, ten years younger, on a couples' retreat? She's having the blast of her life... maybe my mother needs someone younger too." This time I was the one to roll my eyes.

At recess I stood at the window which looked out onto the parking lot. Brad was talking with his friends there. One of the guys playfully pushed him on the chest. His top flew away to reveal a bit of his stomach. My eyes fell on his toned belly, and I imagined my hands touching that perfect six pack. Suddenly he turned toward the window where I was standing, our eyes met. My face felt hot and my heart skipped a beat. I turned away from the window quickly. What I saw didn't surprise me. Carla holding onto Giulio in the corridor. She played the girl with the biggest fish in the pond perfectly, she ran her fingers through her wavy blonde hair, sensuously curling the tips on a finger. *How does she do it? How does she manage to be so confident?* With that thought, I went to buy a packet of Kinder Bueno chocolates.

After class, I found my best friend Natalie waiting for me near the school entrance. "Hey, Nat." I ran towards her, my hands waving in the air.

"What's wrong with you?" Natalie looked at me as if I had just sworn out loud.

"That cute guy is in my class" I whispered, leaning in close to her.

"Who? Which cute guy?" She looked tired as always.

"Do you remember the guy I told you about last year?" I was grinning and dancing on the spot, I couldn't seem to stand still.

"Ah, the one every girl is supposedly after?"

"Yep." I wrapped my arms around her shoulders. "Hey, what are you wearing this time?"

"Favourite outfit, of course." The printed pants she adored were a little worn out, and she was wearing a bright graphic t-shirt with a maxi lemon-yellow grandfather's cardigan. Her braids were secured with a pencil. She definitely had the weirdest outfits!

"Do you think, just because you study art, you have to dress like an artist?" I teased her.

"When one is an artist, one breathes and lives art itself. Picasso lived his art," she raised her voice defiantly.

"Mmmm, I also know that Picasso had *loads* of lovers." I elbowed her in the ribs.

"Well…," my best friend walked away from my prying eyes.

"Hold on, Natalie, you still haven't told me about your summer kiss." I ran-walked after her.

"All I am saying is I am precocious like Picasso."

"Really? You're precocious?" I looked at her Cleopatra like profile. She told me once that some Ghanaian people thought she's Senegalese due to her small nose and very dark skin tone.

"Yep, because Picasso is my best friend?" she grinned showing a perfect set of white teeth.

"*Finta tonta*, don't play dumb with me."

"The other day Josh took some of my paintings for a project at his school and he won a prize." She pretended we were talking about different topic.

"Okay, stop it, I'm not interested in what your brother did with your paintings. I want to know the name, date of birth and address of your summer kiss." She tossed her head back and laughed.

Natalie lived in one of the apartments opposite my house, but it was hard for us to see each other because every afternoon she had to babysit her little brother, Josh. We'd known each other since our diaper days and I'd always thought of her as a saint to be able to live under the same roof as her annoying and rude little brother. Her father worked in one of my grandfather's factories. Natalie was born in Ghana, but her family had moved to Verona when she was nine months old. I loved her to bits and she was always there for me, even if only by phone sometimes.

"But you were saying something about this cute guy," she said as she turned the tables on me.

"Oooh, I can't stand you." I laughed and hugged her.

"That's why we get on so well." She twitched her nose and hugged me back. The roaring of a scooter interrupted her and we both turned to see Brad speeding by on the back of one of his friends' scooters. He nodded in our direction. Natalie came closer to me and in *sotto voce* asked, "Who's that *cutie?*"

"The *cutie* I was just talking about."

"Is he new at your Liceo?" she asked innocently.

"Do you listen to me when I speak?" I stood a few steps back to look at her with my mouth open.

"No." She laughed and carried on walking.

"Nat! You're hopeless." I said as I followed her "Well, he's one of the cool guys on the hockey team. Girls just drop at his feet."

"Are you one of those?" She looked at me from the corner of an eye.

"No way." I felt heat spreading onto my cheeks.

"You should be... he has such a lovely smile." She came closer and touched my forehead with hers.

"Whatever. Don't change the topic. I want to know about your *summer kiss.*"

"Of course you do, *curiosona!*" She smiled. "Okay, I will tell on one condition."

"What?" I beamed.

"Only if we get to the bus stop before those old people." She eyed an elderly couple crossing the zebra lines to the other side of the road.

I ran fast but by the time I got there, the old couple was sitting down on the benches.

"So gullible." Natalie's laughter followed me across the street.

"That. Is. Not. Funny. Why don't you just tell me who your mystery guy is," I begged.

"I have to save my breath to shout at Josh. It's going to be the usual battle to make him do his schoolwork." I knew she was teasing me by the way she curled her nose up.

"Whatever! I shouldn't have to beg you to tell me about you and that guy." I crossed my arms on my chest.

"Oh *amoreeee.*" She patted my shoulder. "*One* of these days I'll tell you. Right now I'm a bit tired."

"I want to kill you." I circled my arms tightly around her shoulders until we were both laughing. Some people waiting for the bus turned to stare at us.

"Typical. Those foreigners. Always making noise." I heard an old woman mutter to herself.

"Boo," I said to her and she jumped on the spot. She grabbed hold of her purse, likely afraid I would rob or beat her, since, from my appearance, I was one of those foreigners.

21

"Susanna," Natalie pinched my arm and looked sternly at me, "don't scare the poor woman. She's right, we foreigners are loud."

CHAPTER 2

Freshly cut lilies sitting in an aquamarine crystal bowl, near the retro dial phone, welcomed me as I entered the hallway. Everything looked so neat. Apart from the sleeping area upstairs, where the walls had different colours in each room to showcase our individual personalities, my house was what Natalie described as straight from a Scandinavian home catalogue with accents of British pop culture. White wooden floor, colourful expensive artworks displayed on the clean white walls. Carefully selected furniture on which flea market items can be found. It was the kind of house with brightness even during foggy, grey Verona winters. However, sometimes all that whiteness and cleanness made me feel out of place because I wanted to be able to leave my shoes around the house without guilt.

"I'm home", I called out as I took my school bag off my shoulders and hung it up in the coat cupboard. The cupboard was a cool feature in the hallway; when it was closed, one saw a big print of a British telephone booth, a clever way to give colour to a boring white area.

"In here," my mother's voice came from the sitting room. I found her on the green velvet sofa overlooking the garden. The clock on the tv read one thirteen-two under the chubby face of Maurizio Costanzo, who was talking about a scoop regarding the top Mafia family in Sicily. But my mother's attention was directed to *Gente*, a popular Italian magazine. I sat on the arm of the sofa, she put the magazine down and reached up to kiss me on the forehead "How was school?"

"Fine." I shrugged, pulled my hair back and relaxed my head on the wall.

"Lunch is in the oven." She indicated the kitchen next door with her head.

"Okay, first I'm going upstairs to Linda" my only and favourite sister. She was about to leave home for university in Milan and I wanted to spend every free second with her

"She's upstairs, packing. Have your lunch now, okay?" my mother insisted

"In a sec. I want to see Linda first." I ran upstairs. I heard music coming out from Linda's room. Without knocking, I let myself in. The spacious room was filled with mementos of her musical achievements. She was intent in packing some CDs. She wore a pair of red leggings and a long, dark blue shirt. Her wild curls pulled into untidy ponytail. She swayed her eighteen-year-old log lean body to the music. I'd never told her but I was so proud to be her sister. Every time I looked at her, the 1996 Miss Italia, Denny Mendez, came to mind. I remembered how during the election, two judges commented that a black woman couldn't represent Italian beauty. I was thrilled to see their sour faces when Mendez was crowned the first Black Miss Italia.

Though Mendez is beautiful, my sister is more beautiful and she could easily win the crown of Miss Italia. *Just imagine Linda on the runway thanking her family, especially me, for sending in her pictures and encouraging her to enter. I should do that one of these days.* I grinned.

"Why that smirk on your face?" Linda looked up at me with her eyebrows raised.

"Oh nothing." I pushed aside some of her clothes and sat on her bed before carrying on. "How many times do you want to pack and unpack and then pack again? You've been packing for the past two weeks."

"Mom told me that when she was going to university she didn't know what to take. In the end she took everything," Linda said in her defence. She and my mom were so similar. They both enjoyed shopping and spending hours in front of a mirror to get their makeup perfect. I was more of a tomboy, always ready to have a laugh and watch soccer games on the television with our father.

Another thing that set me apart from my mother and sister was skincare products. My mother used to say "One expensive cream is better than thousand cheap products."

To which my father would argue back, "All my skin needs is *cheap cocoa butter.*" I agreed with my father and didn't mind using cocoa butter, until one day a girl from the final year told me I smelled like coco and she wanted to bite me. From that moment on, I accepted my mother buying me designer skincare products. The one she chose was light on my skin and didn't spread like batter.

"How was first day of the new school term?" Linda asked, looking up from her CD box.

"Not bad. There's this cute guy in my class."

"How *cute* is he?"

"Sooo cute, he could be the next... I don't know... Johnny Depp?"

"Never!" Linda threw a sock at me. Depp was her

favourite actor and in her opinion no other guy could ever match up.

"I'm telling you. He's so cute Johnny would poop himself if he saw him. Ha. Ha!"

"Liar!" She threw another sock at me. I dodged and fell on the bed, laughing until I couldn't breathe.

"Who are you listening to?"

"Aaliyah Dana Haughton." Linda answered moving her head to the tune.

"She's good." I tried to make conversation with her, struggling to pick among the few topics we had in common. As much as I loved my sister I always felt awkward around her.

"I know." she agreed

"But you're better than her. You can play classic music like nobody else"

"What do you know about music?" she looked doubtfully at me.

It hurt me to hear her say that but I said, "Well, I don't mind listening to the noise you make."

"Thank you very much, *antipatica*." This time her pillow hit me in the head. I laughed.

"I'm going to miss you so much, Lindor." I used the nickname she hated. I was told that when I was little I couldn't pronounce her name properly so I called her Lindor. She tried to correct me but to no avail until I got older and understood the difference. Since then, every time I felt like teasing her I called her Lindor. I think she should be pleased by that because I loved Lindor chocolates.

"Not me. I'm going to Milan to escape your teasing." She smiled, teasing me back.

"Or are you going away to avoid Christian?" I was treading on a very delicate topic; the ex-boyfriend.

"What's Chris got to do with this conversation?" She was visibly annoyed. "I haven't spoken with him for nearly a month."

"Wow, that's the longest you've been off each other." I raised my eyebrows in surprise. "You two were like dry glue. You were no use to anyone."

"Okay, get out of my room, I'm tired." Linda turned away from me.

"Just saying." I shrugged and sat back up on the bed.

"None of your business anyway," her voice was irritated. "Gosh, you don't know anything. Just get out."

"You used to tell me everything." I put a little pout on my face to try to make her feel guilty.

"Look, I don't have time to talk." She motioned her hands at the mess in her bedroom. "Don't you have lunch to eat?" She dismissed me with a little toss of her head.

"If you ever need a shoulder to cry on..." I patted my shoulder then asked, "How is Loredana? You know, your best friend. Christian's brother's girlfriend?"

"I don't know, just get out!" Linda's eyes started to fill up with tears.

"You're not losing anything important. Christian – his face is covered in pimples," I said to recoup to my impertinence. Linda pretended to be busy folding her clothes in the cupboard. Not getting any response back, I carried on "He doesn't know how to dress, he doesn't even want to study. He just works for his father's electrical shop. He'll never amount to anything. At least his older brother, Calvino, is better looking. Lucky Lori."

Linda didn't want to listen to me so she turned up the volume of the stereo. As I turned and left her room, the sound followed me downstairs.

The morning she left for university I sat in my room to cry. I couldn't even say I love you, though love for my favourite sister was burning inside. The rest of September passed without much excitement.

CHAPTER 3

The first Saturday of October Fenice, one of my classmates, celebrated his sixteenth birthday. It was the first party of the season. It was to be a huge affair and it was at his villa, which is in the same neighbourhood as my grandparents' villa. I loved going there, and seeing the beautiful panoramic view out over the city of Verona.

The evening of the party, Natalie came to my house to get ready. When she got into my room she sat on the queen bed and took the current issue of *Cioe'* magazine.

"Why are you putting on lipstick?" she asked from my pillow.

"I thought you were reading that *Cioe'* magazine." I turned to glare at Natalie

"No, I am watching your beauty routine. Since when do you wear lipstick?" Natalie rested her chin on one arm "You've never been so vain."

"Brad asked me if I'm going to the party tonight." I smiled, feeling the butterflies in my stomach. Since the time Brad stood up for me we've started making small talk. He was very friendly with me.

"Ahhh, now you tell me!" Natalie sat back and returned reading the magazine with a pout.

"Is this colour too bright?" I looked at myself critically in the mirror.

"What?" Natalie observed me carefully from head to

toes, as if I was a statue she was painting.

"The lipstick, what else? Is it too fiery?" I rolled my eyes at her

"No," she raised the magazine in the air for a fraction. "Really, Brad asked you?"

"Yes..." I paused for effect.

"How did that happen?" Natalie's tightened smile told me that she wanted to play my game.

"I was minding my own business in Art class, drawing a bowl of dry fruit this morning." Natalie's eyes beamed at at my mention of drawing. "The next thing I remember is his husky voice saying, *'Hey!'* then he flashed me his dimples. I almost died on the spot. I always forget the effect his dimples have on me. Luckily he carried on, asking, *'Why are you ignoring me lately?'*

"What did you say?" Natalie put my *Cioe'* magazine on my bedside table and crossed her legs on the bed.

"Nothing. I smiled at the pages in front of me to avoid staring at him. It's not true that I've been ignoring him." I shrugged, stood up and ironed down my top with my hand. "Then he said, *'Don't ignore me tonight at Fenice's party.'*

"He must like you." Natalie confirmed her theory by shaking her head in affirmation.

"Yeah, right. As if!"

"No, I am serious. He's making an effort with you." Natalie was smiling as she said this.

"What do you know?"

"Well, since this summer I know one or two things."

"Do. Not. Tease!" I pulled down the long sleeves of the

sequin top I was wearing with a pair of bell bottom jeans. "Brad is the most popular guy in the school. What would he want to do with me?"

"Well, you're beautiful, Susanna, and tonight you're going to be the queen of the party." Natalie looked straight into my eyes. "Look at me, I'm not dressed up at all."

"Maybe being an artist gives you a deep insight into beauty." I moved to my cupboard. Suddenly, I felt shy. But she didn't see my expression.

"Now, who's teasing?"

"Well, if I'm going to be the queen, then I can't let my best friend look like one of my servants." I brought out a pleated skirt I'd bought in Scotland the previous summer, and handed it to her. "You can borrow this if you like."

"Thank you, my queen." She teasingly bowed and winked at me.

By the time my father drove us to Fenice's villa, the party was in full swing. From the street we could hear Vasco Rossi's rusty voice blasting out *Vita Spelicolata*. I heard splashing and people screaming the lyrics from the swimming pool in the backyard. My grandparents' villa was just three blocks away and I wondered if the noise reached that far. They had probably been in bed since half past eight.

"Vasco is always popular, even if he's older," Natalie shouted at me over the noise.

"He'll still be giving concerts even when he has a walking stick." I laughed.

31

Some guys were racing up the hill on their Vespas, their front wheels raised off the ground in a cat walk. Other motorbikes were parked in front of the villa as if on display. A shiny red Vespa caught my eyes.

"Must be Fenice's birthday gift," I said. Natalie took my elbow and hurried us through the hallway, bumping into people as we went.

I recognised a few guys and girls from my liceo, but the others were older, maybe in their twenties. It was scary to know that adults were at the party. When we managed to get through the main door, the first thing I noticed was a couple leaning flat against the *credenza* kissing their faces off. To avoid staring, I concentrated on Fenice's family portrait, which hung majestically on the wall leading into the living room. His dad was an elderly, well-groomed man. His mother was the same age as my mother, but she looked skinnier than usual. I knew her because she's my mother's childhood friend. Fenice's younger sister, a chubby twelve year old, was holding their little Chihuahua. With all those freckles, both she and Fenice looked a lot like their mother. In the living room, couples were entangled like snakes slithered on the sofa. Others stood at the foot of the staircase embracing tightly.

I recognised Elisabetta, a girl from Spanish class. She was leaning closely into a guy that looked nearly double her age. He had a beer in one hand and the other hand resting on Elisabetta's waist. It felt like a scene from *Dirty Dancing*.

"Let's get out of here; I don't want us to be the odd ones out." I made an horrified face at Natalie. She let out a laugh and followed me into the back garden.

We found Carla and Giulio there, exchanging tongues. When we got closer, Carla stepped in front of Giulio like she wanted to hide something. "Hey Susanna, how long have you been here?" She ran her fingers over her lips, then through her hair.

"Hi, Giulio, hiding something?" I said, but he frowned at me so I turned to Carla. "Have you seen Ambra," I asked Carla. Ambra was Fenice's girlfriend of six months. She was the mastermind behind the party. I liked her because she was mixed-race like me. Her mother was Ethiopian and her father Italian.

"I saw her upstairs kicking some guys out of one of the bedrooms." She tucked her hair behind her ears. "We came out here because it's mayhem inside." Carla shook her hair, ran her fingers through it again. "*Well*, good luck finding Ambra."

Can't you stop playing with your hair for once? I thought but instead I said, "Nat? What do you think, shall we leave the lovebirds in their nest?"

As I turned to leave, my eyes fell on Brad. He was just stepping into the garden. He was with two older guys I'd never seen before. One of them pointed at me, said something to Brad, and laughed. My eyes caught Brad's and I raised my hand, but he looked away. I turned to Natalie, my lips curled down.

"Isn't that Brad?" She whispered quietly into my ear.

"Yeah."

"I know those guys."

33

"Who are they?" my curiosity span to its peak.

"I'll tell you later." her grip on my arm tightened.

"Why not now?"

"That's William." She hissed, and I swear I could hear her heart drumming against her chest. The guy approaching was a cute, olive-skinned teen wearing a pair of black plastic glasses, a dark blue shirt and marino jeans.

"Hi, Nat, I didn't know you'd be here." He touched Natalie softly on the shoulder, stooped to kiss her, but stopped when he realized I was watching. "Sorry, didn't mean to be rude, I'm William."

"Susanna. Nice to meet you."

"Natalie, you didn't tell me you were coming to this party." William smiled sweetly at my friend.

"Neither did you, and anyway Ambra invited Susanna and said she could bring a friend. I go everywhere she goes, so here I am," Natalie said, arms folded on her chest.

"You never phoned me." He wrapped Natalie's shoulders with his arm. Natalie looked down to avoid my inquisitive eyes. She was giggly, and she looked as if she had seen her favourite artist of all time. Her usual *nothing bothers me* attitude was nowhere to be seen. Then it hit me. William was Natalie's summer kiss that I'd been dying to know more about.

"Guys," I tapped on Natalie's shoulder, "I'm off to look for Ambra." William turned and signaled to his friend that he should carry on. In that fraction, I managed to whisper to Natalie, "I'm going to squeeze all the answers about William out of you later." She smiled and waved me off.

Back inside, the crowd seemed to have doubled in size. I found Ambra drinking punch in the kitchen. "Here you are. I've been looking for you everywhere."

As we hugged, I noticed delicious platters of finger food lined up on the kitchen table. Little kebabs of lamb, tiny fudges, yogurt-coated strawberries and mini eggs filled with pureed black olives. The drinks were chilling in a chic window box filled with chunks of ice. Everything looked straight out of a food magazine. In the corner of the kitchen, a gigantic chocolate fountain poured out white and dark chocolate syrup.

"This spread looks amazing; it reminds me of my grandparents' chef's party meals," I said getting closer to the chocolate fountain.

"Thanks. It took me the whole week to organise all this. I'm so tired." Ambra yawned, "Also, I've been trying to prevent people from trashing the house, but nothing I say or do is helping." The party was really creating a mess. Some guys were throwing potatoes chips at each other in the kitchen and another guy was pushing a second one inside the fridge. But even though some people were literally washing their faces in the chocolate fountain, I couldn't resist dipping some strawberries into the sweet brown mess and stuffing my own face.

I was still in the kitchen eating when I saw William going outside with Natalie. I was going to ask her what time we should get going home, but I couldn't because my mouth was full and I was enjoying the food too much to care about leaving.

I finally went in search of Natalie when it was our curfew, but I couldn't find her anywhere. I found Ambra, who was slow dancing with Fenice. I pulled her aside and said "I can't find Natalie. I don't know what to do. I told my parents we'd find a ride home."

"No worries, I'll find someone to take you."

I was sitting on the steps outside the villa waiting, when Ambra and Fenice came out "Look who's taking you home." My heart slammed like a hammer.

"Brad!" Ambra rested her hand on Brad's shoulder. I shrugged, stood and pulled my curls back from my face. "You don't seem happy," Ambra observed.

"I'm just tired."

"Well! Brad is so kind to take you home." Ambra patted his shoulder. I swear I saw his head double in size. *Yeah right. He wants to show off his Vespa.*

"Thanks, then." I was steaming inside from how he ignored me at the beginning of the evening. "Fenice, thanks for the lovely party."

"You're welcome." Fenice hugged me.

"Ambra, thanks for getting me a ride."

"You should thank Brad. He offered." She winked and blew a kiss our way.

"Do you know where I live?" I asked Brad when Ambra and Fenice left us.

"Show me on the way."

"It's the house opposite the new block of flats, near the

antique shop."

"Are you close to hotel Leopardi?" He smiled and *those* killer dimples appeared. Against my will, a smile escaped my lips.

"Yes. How do you know?"

"I was the receptionist at the hotel this summer. I saw you a couple of times." He said through the helmet.

"Oh, you've been stalking me."

"There's nothing to do in that job but observe the outside world." He handed me an extra helmet and jumped onto the seat. "Hold on tight", he shouted over the roaring engine. *Oh gosh, that smile again.* I wrapped my arms tightly around his waist. When I saw some of the cheerleaders watching, I rested my head on his back and smelled the wonderful pine scented cologne he always wore. He nodded to them and we rode away in the night.

CHAPTER 4
Verona, Italy, March 2000

The chattering outside Susanna's room wakes her up. Still in a hospital bed. Being in the hospital hasn't help her lose the extra weight she needs to lose. She looks at her big belly and sighs. The sound her stomach is making bothers her tonight. Lately, she's been counting stars to force herself to sleep. She feels as if her body has been set on sensitive; she wakes up at the slightest noise. Since her fall, she hasn't been able to stop the tears. The sleep has now cleared from her eyes. She finds a piece of paper in the drawer and begins to write.

04-03 5:50am

I've been in this psychiatric hospital for two days. Two days of doing nothing. Apart from sitting with a bunch of skinny girls in the common room. Looking at them makes me hate myself even more. There is one girl everyone calls "Trigger" and she wears clothes that show too much skin. Her dark blonde hair is brushed to perfection. Every time she comes into the common room, she has makeup on. She's very slender but not as skeletal as some of the other girls. I observe her every move when I find myself in her company. One thing I admire about her is how she eats her meals without complaining or playing with the food. I wonder how she can eat and still be skinny.

They say I need to increase my sugar levels. For this they've put me on the drips. These days I look forward to having the needle put into my arm. I would have gone mad by now if it wasn't for that. Life inside the hospital is so boring. We repeat the same routine every day. Wake up, weigh in, shower, breakfast, group therapy, free time, lunch, lesson, snack, reading time, dinner, group activity, bed. Maybe the order is not exactly that but who cares now. Mom's coming this morning to talk to the director of the hospital. I want to get out of here, but I'm freaking out since I don't know what he's going to tell her. I just need to be out of this place ASAP. I need to lose some pounds. I am so bloated. Gosh, I want to cut off my "love handles!" I hate them!

Olga Danso, Susanna's mother, walks into the hospital hall. She shakes the rain off her umbrella and puts it in the plastic holder at the entrance. She runs her fingers through her wet, wavy brown hair. The crick crack of her shoes can be heard down the corridor.

"*Ciao, darling.*" She greets Susanna with a broad smile as she pushes the door open. Susanna doesn't smile. She sits up on the bed, a frown on her face. She recoils when her mother wraps her shoulders with an arm. "How are you feeling today? Today the doctor will tell me when you can come home." Olga continues smoothing her daughter's curls. "You will be fine; you know that, don't you?"

"I *am* fine!" Susanna hisses not looking at her mother.

"I know *Susina*, I know..." Susanna scans the clinical white walls. The word *Susina* rings in her ears. *I am not a plum, I am not a plum, I am not a plum.* She chants inside her head. She looks out the window, where the rain drums the roof like falling needles.

"I don't like it when you call me *Susina*." Susanna clutches to the bed covers, digging her nails into her palm.

"You've been our *Susina* since you were a tiny baby. You were so cute with your chubby cheeks." Olga's smile is warm but it bothers Susanna.

"It means *plum*!" Susanna says.

"I don't mean it in a nasty way. It is just a small version of Susanna." Olga organizes some books on the desk.

"I am sixteen years old, mom. Old enough not to be a Susina!"

"*Cara!...*"

"Can you stop calling me *darling*, I don't like being called *susina or cara*. Full Stop."

"But Susina." Olga's big smile is now replace by a tight smile.

"I don't *like it*! Find another nickname if you insist on nicknames." Susanna says and looks straight in her mother's eyes. In that moment a nurse pops her head at the door.

"Signora Danso, the doctor is ready for you." The nurse consults the clipboard in her hand, then continues, "Susanna, you can come too." Susanna hides her hand in her pocket when her mother tries to hold it. She clasps her jumper when they get out of her room. They follow the rubber crocs of the slim nurse down the hall. Just the thought of another day enclosed in that hospital makes Susanna want to purge. *God, I hate being here!* Her mother wraps her arms around her shoulders. This time Susanna doesn't reject the embrace.

"You can sit here, Susanna" the nurse indicates a chair outside the doctor's office.

"Are you going to be okay, darling?" Olga pulls back one of Susanna's falling curls.

"Hmmm." Her daughter grunts. Olga caresses her cheek.

"You see, *signora...* hmmm ... Dan ... su.." the doctor begins as soon as Olga arrives in his office.

"Danso, it's pronounced *Danso.*" She brushes her hair with her hand and smiles.

"Mmm, based on a series of examinations your daughter's current BMI is 17.9." He wipes his face with a hand, "It's considered underweight."

"We see she is losing weight, but why?"

"It can be caused by stress and overload of school activities." The doctor slouches on his office chair as if annoyed with the whole world. "From the analysis there is nothing to worry about. Yes, Susanna has lost weight, but she can bounce back. Okay?"

Olga lets out a sign of relief, then says "This is her final year of junior high."

"Nothing to worry about then. Exam pressure can decrease a person's appetite." The doctor clicks something on his computer, then he smiles and says "All she needs is to improve her eating habits, sleep well and relax. Soon she will bounce back."

"We were worried sick," Olga tells the doctor.

"I can imagine, being a parent myself. My daughter is a few years younger than yours." The doctors stands up and walks towards the door. He takes his filthy glasses off to clean them.

"We'll make sure she eats." Olga follows him. At the door she reaches her hand out to the doctor. "Thank you again."

"You're welcome and remember to let her eat well, sleep well and relax plenty." The doctor shakes Olga's hand. He opens the door and continues. "Hmmm... she just has to eat a little more pasta and she will be fine in few days," he jokes. Susanna gets up to stand next to her mother. Her eyes fall on the doctor's name tag, Tavernello. His surname is the same as a cheap Italian wine.

"*What a beautiful, dark skinned girl,*" Doctor Tavernello says, raising his hand up towards Susanna's face. Since her nursery days, she has always hated being touched on the cheek. That gesture takes her back to when the other kids' mothers would pinch her cheeks, calling her *cute darkie*. This time she doesn't allow the doctor to go further, Susanna slaps his hand away from her face, she turns and walks away from him and her mother.

"Susanna ..." Olga says, shocked. She apologizes to the doctor and then briskly walks after her daughter.

Outside, it's still raining. The air smells fresh.

"Why did you do that?" Olga asks her daughter once they are in the car driving on the highway.

Susanna doesn't answer. Instead, she concentrates on the red car in front of them. There are two children sitting at the back pushing each other. Their mother turns and says something pointing her finger at the girl, who looks older. The little boy sticks out his tongue.

"I asked you a question ... Susanna? Why did you slap the doctor's hand?"

Susanna puffs out her cheeks. "He wouldn't allow his own daughter to be touched by a stranger."

"He was trying to be nice." Olga looks at Susanna.

"*I* don't want people to be nice to me ..." Susanna returns her mother's gaze, noticing more wrinkles around her eyes. She turns back to the road and continues, "Am I beautiful because I am *beautiful*? Or am I beautiful because I look different?"

"You are gorgeous without any conditions ... but for some people your colour is so beautiful they like pointing that out." Susanna turns back to the street. The red car is in the slow lane. The little boy looks in her direction and pulls a mean face at her. Susanna shows him her middle finger. The boy calls his mother, but his sister laughs and mimics *thanks*! Susanna smiles back and quickly turns before the boy's mother can catch her eyes. Olga drives fast past the red car. Now in front of them, a sporty blue car is trying to overtake another grey car, but the other driver doesn't slow down.

"He wouldn't have touched a white girl," Susanna says. Her mother doesn't respond to this last comment. Susanna continues. "He was about to touch my cheek because he thinks I am next to nothing."

"Susanna? Don't say that." Olga turns to Susanna with her lips pursed together.

"Does skin tone define beauty? Are you beautiful because you are beautiful or because you are a beautiful *white* girl? Aren't you just beautiful? I don't hear people complimenting you by defining your skin tone. Why do people always put me into a skin tone box? Don't you just live life? Do people question what kind of human being are you? Aren't I just a normal girl? Why, why do I have to be classified as black or white?" Susanna tastes the salty tears but doesn't try to wipe her face.

"Don't fret, *Cara*. I love you so much, the whole family loves you so, so much you can't imagine. We all have to go through the teenage years. It's difficult but you will find the answer." Susanna wishes her family's love was enough to make her love herself.

04-03-2000

I don't know where to begin. I am FAT. They fed me like a porco. I hate them. They don't get it! They don't get it! They, my parents, nurses and doctors. All I need is to be left alone. I didn't need to be in that cell! What were they thinking? Whoever phoned the ambulance is an asshole...

Susanna hears some steps, she hides the diary and pen under the pillow just in case. She hears someone outside her door, but no-one knocks or enters. She breathes again, then brings the diary from under the pillow and carries on in a quick scrawl.

My parents are watching me. It's not funny! They want to take all my rights away. How can I lose the last 2 kilos? I just weighed myself — I have to lose FIVE, 5 kilos or almost eleven pounds. How can I lose all that weight? OMG, I am so depressed! I wouldn't be writing this depressing entry if I hadn't gone to that hospital. I would have lost the extra weight I need to lose to be perfect for Brad. I would have been happy by now!

Susanna puts down the diary, she goes to weigh herself.

I just weighed myself and guess what? I'm 120.15 pounds. That means I have to lose more than I just wrote. I have to start school tomorrow and I'm worried, I don't know what people are going to say. I must dress to kill. Maybe I'll wear my new jeans, my mother is going to monitor my meals like a prisoner guard. I have to find a way to avoid eating the whole plate, like I was doing until last Saturday. The weather forecast says tomorrow is going to be warm again. I will wear something loose just in case ... hmmm... I'm feeling bloated, I better go check the scale again.

CHAPTER 5
Verona, Italy, October 1999

It felt wonderful, sitting behind Brad with the wind caressing my face. I rested my head on his shoulders. He smelled like forest rain. At each red traffic light he turned a little to make sure I was still behind him.

"Are you comfortable?" he asked.

"Yes." *I wish the light could stay red forever.* He smiled, watching for the red light to turn green. Too soon, he was parked in front of my gate. My mother, who had probably been standing near the window since eleven o'clock, came out.

"Susanna?" She wrapped the mint coloured shawl she had around her shoulders.

"I'll be in in just a second." *How embarrassing!*

"Is that your sister?" Brad asked while he removed his helmet.

"Are you kidding me? She is my mom!"

"She looks young, that's all."

"Well, thanks for the ride." I handed him the borrowed helmet.

"You are welcome..." He hesitated a little bit before saying, "Did you enjoy the evening?"

"I did. How about you?" I tried not to look surprised

"It was okay, but it could have been better if I'd seen you sooner." He smiled, looking searchingly into my eyes.

"Really, you didn't see me?" This time I could feel my eyes opening too wide.

"No, when did you get there?" He hung the helmet on a hook under the seat.

"I was there when you arrived with those guys." I stared at him to see how he reacted to that.

"Which guys." He looked relaxed.

"The bald guys"

"Bald guys? Hah, the guys with short hair. I didn't see you." He didn't move his eyes from mine.

"Even when I was waving to you like mad?" I folded my arms on my chest.

"Nope." The way he looked straight into my eyes didn't make me want to doubt him "I didn't see you. I mean it."

"Oh... well, I went outside to look for somebody. Maybe that's why you didn't notice me. What did you do the whole night then?" I sat on the sidewalk

"I was by the pool," he said sitting next to me.

"I suppose you were chatting up more girls..."

"Not really, I was just sitting there when Ambra came to talk to us."

"Hard to believe." I rested my head on my knees and looked at his perfect profile.

"Why?" He turned to look at me

"Well, for one thing, you are the cutest guy in the whole school. Girls are practically *dying* to kiss you." I bit my lip because I didn't want him to think I was one of them but it was too late.

"Really? I didn't know that girls are dying to kiss me," He put his face closer to mine. "Are you one of those girls?"

"Of course not." I turned away from him. He touched one of my rebellious curls. I was surprised that Brad was flirting with me like that. For the past two weeks he had been distant with me, and though his previous actions had hurt me, flirting with him now lifted my heart.

"*Bugiarda.* You're lying. Are you sure you don't want to kiss me?" I turned back to him, my heart drumming as if at a

Brazilian Carnival feast. I didn't move an inch. He moved closer; still I didn't do anything to stop him. I was excited to have him so close to me. His breath, reminding me of toast and jam, caressed my face. "So, how do you feel now?" he took hold of my chin.

I looked down, my heart thudding in its place. I kept inspecting the ground, saying nothing.

"Don't you want to kiss me," he asked again, and this time he wrapped his arms around me.

I broke from the embrace and stood up. *Of course I would like to kiss you, stupid.* I backed up onto the pavement. He was playing a silly game with me and I didn't like it.

"Oh, Susanna? Don't take it badly. You know what?" He bounced back onto his feet.

"What?"

"I really like you."

"Guess what, I don't like *you*, so thanks for the ride and goodnight." I turned my back on him and walked down the path that led to my front door. Once inside, I went to the window to check out what Brad was up to. He was putting his helmet back on. He was not looking at my house.

"Susanna?" my mother called from the living room.

I jumped around. "Yes, Mom." I hurried to the living room where she was watching the midnight news.

"Who was that boy?" the shawl was on her legs.

"That was Brad from my class."

"And where is Natalie?" she pulled the shawl off as she got off the sofa.

I shrugged. She looked at me inquisitively and shook her head. She seemed resigned but I didn't worry about it. I wanted to be alone to think about Brad.

CHAPTER 6

The rays pouring through the shutters of my windows woke me up on Sunday morning. I turned to my table clock, it was eleven o'clock and my parents were out for a jog.

I stayed in bed a few more minutes enjoying the light. I loved Sundays, especially when it was sunny and my room was full of sun. When it reflected on the yellow walls it made me feel as if I was swimming in sand dune. But what I loved the most was the fact that there was no school.

I went to soak myself in the bath. I closed my eyes and relaxed my head on a bath pillow for an hour. After putting on some comfortable clothes, I prepared myself a delicious breakfast: two pieces of toast, strawberry jam, a bowl of cornflakes and a glass of juice. When my parents were around, I couldn't eat in the living room because my Mom thought it wasn't civilized. Because they were not around, I took my tray into the living room, turned on my favourite music channel and enjoyed my healthy breakfast.

I must have dozed off because I didn't hear my parents coming into the house.

"Susanna? How many times do I have to tell you?" my mom's sharp voice woke me up

"What?" I asked sat up on the sofa. She was pointing her finger at the tray next to me. "Oh, that? Sorry, Mom."

"Sorry doesn't cancel your behaviour." she seemed quite cross.

"Olga, it's okay." My dad intervened.

"Nelson, that's not right. I've told her many times, but she doesn't listen."

"Sorry, Mom. Really am sorry, Mom."

"Well, maybe this time you will listen." She took the tray to the kitchen. My dad kissed her as she passed and winked. She smiled. I loved to see them so much in love.

My dad started his usual soccer sermon whenever he wanted me to watch the game, something he did every Sunday. Just then the phone rang, I jumped up and ran into the hallway to grab the receiver.

"Hello?" I asked in short voice

"*Hey*, Susah, how are you?" It was a nice to hear my sister's voice.

"Linda! I am fine, you?" I sighed heavily to catch breath.

"What's wrong?" her voice sounded so grown up.

"Nothing, just running." I said then asked "What are you up to?"

"Lying on my bed – "

"Watching the ceiling and composing music in your head?" I continued for her.

"How do you know?"

"You're my sister, remember that?"

"Mmmmm. The sun is shining and I wish I was home."

"What's that I hear?"

"The song I am composing."

"I should come visit you before you go mad."

"You are annoying like all little sisters, but I miss you the same."

"Me too."

"How was the party last night?"

"I had so much fun. Guess who I saw last night."

"Who?"

"No, I didn't see Christian if you were wondering. I'm sorry I don't know much about what he is up to these days. I saw Marco instead."

"Loredana's little brother?"

"Yes, so I didn't see Christian." I heard Linda clearing her throat.

"How many times do I have to tell you before you get it." She paused for a second "I don't care about him. Rather tell me, did you kiss anyone interesting?"

"You silly! Well, if you want to know. Brad, the cutest guy in the school, took me home on his new red Vespa."

"Lucky you." After a pause she asked, "Is Mom there?"

"In the shower – Ah, here is she. Mom? Linda's on the phone." My mother had walked into the hall at that moment, her wet brown curls hanging loose on her shoulders. I really thought she looked beautiful. After two daughters, Mother Nature still graced her with an enviable body. I looked at my loose jeans and loose top and wished I had a sense of style, like her and Linda.

"Talk to you soon, lil' sister. Come visit me." Linda cheered up.

"I love you. Don't think about. You know who –"

"I won't – kisses! *Ciao.*" I could tell she was annoyed,

maybe it was time I stopped teasing her about her ex.

"My kiss and *ciao* are bigger than yours."

"Girls, enough."

"Okay, Olga."

"Your sister doesn't listen." I heard Mom say to Linda.

A few minutes later, she walked into the living room. She looked worried, but I didn't want to bother her with questions. Instead, I went to phone Natalie.

"Hello?" The voice on the other line sounded tired.

"Natalie, it's midday. Don't tell me you are still sleeping?"

"Mmm, no…" She yawned.

"Tell me, where did you disappear to with William last night?" I put on my detective voice.

"Shhhhh! If my parents ask you who I went home with, you know what to say," she hissed.

"I would but, unfortunately for you, my mother saw me with Brad last night." I was so excited to say Brad's name it came out a bit louder than I wanted.

"Brad?" suddenly Natalie sounded wide awake

"Don't change subject. I want to know about you and William!" I wanted to tell her so much about Brad but my curiosity prevailed.

"What time can I see you?" she asked.

"This afternoon. In fact why don't you ask your dad and brother if they'd like to watch the game over here? They'll save me from watching it with my dad."

"Wait a second." I heard Natalie speaking in Ghanaian. I really liked the way her voice sounded when she spoke in her native language. I envied the fact that she could speak

Italian, Ghanaian and English. I'd always wanted to learn Ghanaian, but my father only spoke English with us.

Natalie returned to the receiver.

"My dad's okay with that but Josh can't come 'cause he's grounded." She let out a laugh.

"See you later then. I'll tell my dad you're coming over. About four?"

"See you."

When Natalie and her father arrived later that afternoon, I took her by the hand and rushed upstairs, closing the bedroom door behind us.

"You are my prisoner. You will be freed after I hear the whole truth about you and William." I laughed

"Really? – It's so embarrassing." She threw herself onto my bed and fanned her face.

"Do you want me to open the window?" I made it to the window as I said, "I'm not having any of your dramatic tricks."

"Okay, no need to open the window – if I can't escape!" she sighed and said, "Promise you'll not tell *anyone*."

I lied down next to her on the bed and said, "Scout's honour." I figuratively zipped my lips.

"Alright then." she got off the bed and went to open my door to make sure nobody was out there. When she returned to the bed she began, "When you were in Scotland this summer, I went to a Sunday afternoon club."

"An afternoon club?" I'd heard of that but had never

been to one.

"Sorry, I forgot that you've never been to an afternoon club. It's just a club where the majority are all young guys, sixteen to twenty-one years old."

"How did you manage to hide that from your Mom?" I looked at her, puzzled. I continued saying, "Didn't she say you have church to go to? Don't tell me about that. Go on with the story."

"Well, I told her I was going to a new church with a couple of friends." I watched her as she cleaned a fluff off the bed.

"Natalie, why the lies?" Natalie's mom, being a strict Christian, never allowed my friend to do anything other than go to school, do house chores and hang out with me.

"I know, I know... I feel terrible about the lies."

"I don't know what to do with you," I jokingly said.

"Well, at the club I met two guys. To identify them I will use A and B." She bit her nails "They came with two different groups. I was dancing, minding my own business, when A came to introduce himself. He's nineteen years old."

"Wow, nineteen? This is getting intriguing."

"Yep. Plus, he looks like a surfer, long wavy brown hair."

"Really? Oh. My. God."

"I was walking around the club when I literally bumped into B. He was standing at one of the entrances to the dance floor, I thought he looked cute." She stopped talking, took off her blue sweater. "Okay..." She bit her upper lip "That evening I kissed A."

"What? You tell me just like that?" I went onto my

elbows to look at her. She avoided my eyes

"Okay, so, well, later on in the afternoon, toward the evening, I saw A again. It was so hot and he offered me a drink. You know one thing led to another." She pulled her braid onto one side.

"Was he a good kisser?"

"Compared to the few guys I've kissed, he's not that great" I shook my head. She smiled and then said, "At the end of the evening I met B again."

"And you kissed him"

"Noooo, we exchanged telephone numbers." Natalie relaxed her head on the bed.

"Did you give him your real number?"

"Of course not. My mom would kill me."

"Did you get A's number?"

"No... well, I didn't really like him. I guess, I let him kiss me because he was so cute and sort of charming too." She hid her face in the pillow.

"Oh Natalie! You are naughty." I poked her on the shoulder

"I guess the heat went to my head?" she looked away from the pillow. I hugged her. She pulled her braids into a ponytail.

"Anyway, the following day, B, who is William, invited me out." A big smile appeared on her lips.

"How did he get your number?" I was so excited to finally hear more about my friend's summer love story.

"From one of the girls"

"Ah, and your mom?"

"Luckily, I picked up when he phoned." She hid her eyes behind her fingers as she told me what happened next. "He invited me out. On the day of the date, I was waiting for him near the bookshop in *piazza*, when I saw him together with A, whose name is Arthur."

"Oh no!"

"My heart felt like jumping out of my chest, I was so scared, but I was quick enough to hide behind a shelf."

"What about William?"

"I didn't want to see both of them at the same time, so I stood him up."

"Really? Poor William."

"I know, I felt so bad." I knew my friend well enough to understand that she meant it

"Oh, Natalie." I circled her shoulders with one arm.

"Don't worry. He told me that Arthur is his half-brother."

"Why were you so worried? Thank God, I am too young to become aunt."

"Su!" She pushed me "Seriously, what do you take me for? I thought kissing two brothers was bad enough. Pregnant? Me? Never, my mom would kill me."

"You didn't know, did you?"

"What?"

"That they are brothers?"

"They look similar, but it didn't cross my mind then."

"Well, well, well how about you and William now?"

"He asked me out again!"

"Shall I call you Natalie the *conquistador*?"

"*No*! Just tell me about you and Brad instead."

"You said you were going to tell me about the guys he was with."

"Nothing important. I heard they are part of a group."

"Which group?"

"Mmmm, the Blue something... I don't remember the exact name. But I heard they're racists. But I'm sure it's not true. Did something happen with him?"

"Who?"

"Brad, of course."

"Nothing. He teased me, saying I wanted to kiss him."

"Maybe he likes you –" Natalie winked at me.

"Really, Natalie? I mean, do you think the hottest guy in school would want me as a girlfriend, when Camilla, the other bombshell, apart from Carla, recently became available? Of course not!"

"Why not?" Natalie asked, but I couldn't answer because the noise coming from downstairs interrupted me

"GOAAAAAAAL"

"I think our team scored! We better go downstairs!" I said and got off the bed.

Halfway down, Natalie whispered "Su, don't tell your mom. She might tell my mom by mistake and you know, she'll freak out."

"My word is sacred." I wrapped my arms around her shoulders as we made our way downstairs.

CHAPTER 7

Monday morning was raining when I woke up. I hoped it would stop soon but it was still wet by the time Mom dropped Natalie and me in front of my school. As soon as I got out of the car, I opened my rainbow umbrella, which always cheered me up but not that morning. Natalie squeezed my shoulders and whispered good luck. Since she had sowed into my head the idea that Brad might like me, my mind had his beautiful hazel eyes printed on a billboard. I'd spent most of Sunday evening thinking about Brad and what had happened, or more like what didn't happen, between us on Saturday when he'd brought me home.

"Natalie, I'm sure it's nothing." I brushed my hair onto one side.

"Good luck anyway." She gave me a kiss on the cheek.

"Thank you." *Surely Natalie's artistic imagination is way ahead of us.* I thought as I hurried into class before the second bell went off. I sat at my desk, brought out my French exercise book. I absent-mindedly turned pages until I saw Brad from my peripheral vision coming into class. I focused on the page in front of me but I didn't register anything because he sat behind me. His rain forest smell took me back to Saturday night when I'd lain my head on his shoulder as he rode his scooter to my house. I didn't say anything but I was dying to hear his voice.

"Hello?" He finally said. I jumped on the spot as his

breath brushed my neck, I felt the tingling rising inside. I turned to him and he asked in his husky voice, "How was your weekend?"

"Mmm, goo, good, good." I stuttered "Thanks for asking." My voice was nowhere near audible. He leaned on my chair for few more seconds, maybe expecting *conversation*? But then he sat back because I didn't say anything. I found it hard to follow French lesson that day. The rain dribbling down the window panes and Brad's eyes on me pulled me into a world of fairies.

"Susanna Danso!" Prof. Cazzanella's rough voice rose a little before I could hear him. "Can you grace us with your presence on planet Earth? Complete this phrase for me." He stood at my side.

"J'e sui... mmm?"

"Forget it. Pay attention to the lesson, you need it," he said curtly. Everyone started to laugh. Heat spread all over my face and neck. It didn't help when Brad leaned forward *again* to say, "Don't mind old baldy." The heat on my face sky rocketed but I managed to let out a faint laugh, then turned to face him, a smile on my lips. He winked at me. I turned back to my exercise book, my mind full of the possibilities of what it might mean having Brad as my boyfriend. Maybe I knew right there and then that he had won me over. For the rest of the day, anytime I caught his gaze we smiled, while my insides melted a little more.

Even though it was still drizzling, I went home after class feeling like the sun itself. Around four o'clock, while I was upstairs reading *Anne Frank*, I heard the phone ringing downstairs. My mother was out at the beauty spa and my father was still at work. I was very annoyed with whoever was on the other end of the line because I didn't like being disturbed when reading a good novel.

"Helloooo?" I curtly breathed down the receiver.

"Hello? It's Brad... Brad Lawson." His voice was gentle. *How did he get my number?* As if he could read my mind he said, "I asked Ambra for your number."

Ambra is always in the middle, "Can I help?" I kept my enthusiasm in check by not giggling.

"I wanted to say sorry for this morning."

"Sorry for what."

"For Prof. Cazza."

"It wasn't your fault Cazzanella was on my case today. Plus, I was..." I shrugged.

"What?" Brad asked. I put so much into that simple question like *what do you like, what it's to kiss you...* but in the end I simply said "Oh nothing... I didn't sleep well last night, that's all."

"Why?" Brad asked again. I didn't know what he wanted to hear from me. "I was having nightmares."

"Oh! I didn't sleep well myself..." He paused again. I assumed waiting for my response.

"Why?"

"I was thinking about our ride on Saturday."

I felt a big chest of drawers falling on my head. I pinched

myself twice to make sure I was not dreaming. I flinched from the pain and tried to say something but nothing came out.

"Susanna? Are you there?" He sounded worried

"Yes." *Just under a chest of drawers.*

"I really like you." The words arrowed at me.

"What?" I opened my eyes at the phone.

"I said I like you." I couldn't believe what he was saying. I looked at my image in the mirror on the coat cupboard in the hallway. My hair all over my face, bed sheet marks printed on my left cheek. Baggy clothes to hide my body that I didn't particularly like. Now Brad, the coolest guy at Liceo Linguistico Dante Alighieri, was saying he *likes me? Me*, the one everyone teased because I had a big *round* bottom? *Me*, Susanna Danso, oh my, my.... I was still in the whirlpool when Brad said, "Su? Are you still there?" *Su, he calls me Su?* I was sure he knew the effect of his words on me. He knew his status at school.

"I was reading when you phoned," I said but instead thought, *God, don't let me ruin this.*

"Am I disturbing you?" He was quieter than before.

"No, not at all. I just meant.... How about you?" *Really, Susanna, is this all you can come up with?*

"How about me, what?"

"Oh, what were you doing before you called?"

"I was watching a wrestling show my cousin sent me from Canada."

"You have cousins in Canada?" *Small talk, this is better!*

"My dad is from Canada."

"*Che bello.*" How beautiful? *What the hell are you saying, stupid?*

"How about you? Do you like me?"

"I think so … mmmm … yes." I felt my knees weaken under me, I should have sat down when I answered.

"Good..." He sounded pleased. There was a pause before he asked, "Are you really busy?"

"No, not right now, but I wanted to finish my schoolwork."

"You can't come to the piazza then?" It was tempting to send all my plans to hell and meet him in downtown but I didn't want him to think I was desperate, so instead of listening to the big part of my heart which wanted to say, *Oh yes, I will come to the edge of the world with you,* or something ridiculous like that, I said, "Sorry, I can't."

"Pity." The disappointment sounded like a bomb on the receiver.

"I guess we'll see each other tomorrow?" I was burning inside.

"Sure, okay! See you tomorrow, then." His receiver was in the cradle before I could change my mind.

He's offended, I discussed internally as I walked to the living room. *Have I offended him? Does he like me still?* I sat on the nearest sofa for five minutes hyperventilating. I went back to the hallway and composed my best friend's phone number. "Guess what!" I said.

"What?"

"Brad just phoned me." I was glad she couldn't see my face. With my teeth stretched from ear to ear, I looked like a clown in the mirror above the phone.

"Really? What did he say?"

"Guess, guess." My heart was pounding against my chest.

"Help him with his schoolwork?"

"Way off track. Try again?"

"Just tell me. I'm too tired to play, plus I was sleeping when you phoned. Josh isn't at home and I'm having a quiet afternoon." I built up the suspense, inhaled a deep breath then gushed out "BradaskedmeifIwanttobehisgirlfriend."

"Slowdown"

"Brad. Asked. Me. If. I. Want. To. Be. His. Girlfriend." I deliberately took my time.

"Not that slow, but anyways. Did he? Word for word?" I could hear she was surprised.

"No, but... well, he said he *really* likes me. What else does he mean? Oh, Natalie, can you imagine Brad Lawson declaring himself to me?" I bit the nail off my thumb.

"Why not? You're beautiful and if I was a boy I would have asked you out long time ago." Her heartfelt laugh calmed my nerves. I knew she was teasing, but this time I did not complain. I took the compliment and for a moment enjoyed my so-called *beauty*. I never thought of myself as beautiful; although Natalie and Linda kept telling me I was. That afternoon for a moment, just a moment, I believed Natalie.

Natalie yawned on the other side.

"Were you sleeping?"

"Yes, but now that I am wake, I won't go back to sleep."

"Sorry, but I wanted you to be the first to know about

this awesome news."

"Oh, what an honour. What are you going to do tomorrow?"

"I don't know. I better go pick out a nice outfit."

"For tomorrow? Susah, it's not even five!"

"This is a special occasion."

We said our goodbyes and I put the phone down. *What am I going to wear? How should I wear my hair?* In that moment I wished Linda was around to help me dress. I stumbled back into my room. I went through my wardrobe and I pulled out jeans, skirts, tops and dresses, one after the other without finding anything good enough. I ran into Linda's bedroom and *borrowed* a pair of dark blue jeans, paired with a light pink sweater.

CHAPTER 8

Tuesday morning I felt like I was going to sit a life-changing exam. It took me forever to release the tension in my shoulders under the shower. I ran the warm water for more than half an hour. After fussing for a long time over my hair, I decided to pull my curls into a ponytail. I then applied Linda's lip shine. I was in front of the mirror checking the last details when I heard Natalie's voice downstairs speaking to my mom. It was the bus ride to school day.

"Here I am..." I ran downstairs and grabbed my schoolbag without letting my mom see my face "You should eat something." Mom said.

I grabbed the toast to take with me. "See you later, Mom..."

Once outside Natalie teased me. "Hello! Miss Tyra Banks! And look at those blue mocassino shoes. Wow, are you really my friend Susanna, or her clone?"

"Do you like it?" I opened my coat to show her what I was wearing underneath.

"Oolalala ... lucky, this Brad."

"I'm the lucky one!" I hugged Natalie tightly.

"Su, are you okay?"

"More than okay. Nat, I'm over the moon." I hugged her more tightly. I was not okay, really. In that moment I wished Natalie was in the same school as me. I wanted moral support to meet my *"hot* boyfriend." I needed Natalie's warm embrace if the conversation Brad and I had had the previous afternoon was just a dream — but one that felt so real. If it was a dream then her hug was going to comfort me when Brad ignored me and laughed in my face for believing that he'd said he *really* likes me.

"See you after school," I said, letting Natalie out of the embrace once we reached my school.

"See you later, and be strong," she said and gave me a peck on the cheek. My eyes followed her as she walked in the other direction. She looked so secure and aware of the world. A part of me wanted to run after her, to be in her company for the rest of the day. She was like a fortress when I needed a shoulder to lean on. A chill wind blew on my face. I sighed and wrapped my arms around my body, rubbing them through my coat for comfort.

When I opened the front door of the school, the autumn chill followed me inside. Gigi Caravaggio's voice shattered my blissful state: "Susanna, *porno star...*"

My heart jumped into my throat. He was joined by some of the other guys with him singing that horrible song I hated. Brad was nowhere to be seen. "Look at her, today she wants to be a super model... Are you going to cast for *Playboy?* Is it a part for big bottom? With that *culo* you have, you will be picked straight away."

I knew it was too beautiful to be true, I thought trying to ignore Gigi, the kill joy. *It was a dream yesterday afternoon, how could I being so naïve as to believe that Brad and I were going to be a couple?* I was fighting back tears. All the joy I'd felt the night before vanished. In its place, anger and frustration appeared. I was about to say something when I heard his voice behind me.

"Caravaggio... back off..." Brad's arm brushed my shoulder.

"What's your problem?" Caravaggio demanded of Brad. "We're just having a bit of fun"

What Brad said surprised everyone around us. "I'm with her..." My heart leaped back into my stomach as I turned to the person saying those words. I looked up; our eyes met. *I did not dream anything yesterday.* I tried to avoid Caravaggio's eyes. Brad looked down at me. We walked next to each other without saying a word. The chill I'd felt earlier was replaced by summer heat.

Mid-morning recess was one of the worst experiences of my entire academic career, not counting gym classes, of course. I had actually underestimated how many girls were after Brad until that fifteen minutes after our first "public outing".

I felt like a celebrity wearing some of the most talked about designers. The jeans were not too tight and the pink jumper enhanced my dark olive skin. But the reaction was not what I had expected.

"Who does she think she is with her designer clothes? Brad is just with her because he is trying to prove a point..." I overheard some of the girls loudly whispering. I didn't care if Brad was trying to show off. *If he's using me, then I must be*

THEODORA O. AGYEMAN-ANANE

worth something. To be with the best looking guy in the whole school is... well... a dream come true. I smiled at the thought.

"Would you like some?" Brad offered me a piece of his Kinder Bueno, bringing me back into the corridor of Liceo Dante.

"No, thanks! I have my own snack. My mom always makes me take my own just in case the school's snack machine is empty. As if snacks in this big school would ever run out!" *He will think I'm stupid, I'm talking too much.*

"Yeah, parents," Brad murmured. We walked outside to go sit under the big chestnut tree in the parking lot. Some guys from the other class joined us. Caravaggio and another guy stood aside watching us and whispering to one another. I felt bad that I was the cause Brad wasn't talking to some of his friends. I was relieved when Carla and Giulio came to join us.

"The little Susanna, eh... good, good, good..."

"What? Carla, don't –" I said through gritted teeth.

"Uh okay, don't be defensive" she sat down next to me. "You should be happy, you have Brad as your boyfriend."

Being stared at was awful; it made our fifteen minute recess seem longer than usual. There was no formal introduction, but many of the cool guys I didn't hang out with before came to ask Brad something I was not able to hear. On some faces I could read the question, *what is Brad doing with Susanna Big Bottom?* I asked myself the same question. The bell ending the break interrupted my stream of anxious thoughts.

On our way back to the building Brad took my hand in

his. *Oh my, the butterflies again.* I felt drunk with all the attention. My own happiness made me sick. *How did I get so lucky? Of all the guys I dreamt to have as a boyfriend, I never believed Brad Lawson would be the one. He isn't ashamed to be seen with my hand in his.* I thought I'd died and gone to heaven. Bryan Adam's song started to play in my head. Although I was the happiest girl at Liceo Dante, I wanted that school day to finish immediately. I was extremely aware to the point of embarrassment to be seen with Brad, but I couldn't imagine how that day could be better.

"Try this one." He gave me a cream and pink helmet after school. I tried it on; it was perfect.

"How did you know?" I asked.

"That's my mom's old helmet, I couldn't bring my sister's because she's only thirteen. She's just a skinny little thing," Brad concluded with an affectionate note in his last words. "Jump on the back." He laughed and helped me sit behind him.

I was laying my head on Brad's shoulder, enjoying the wind through my curls, when I suddenly realized that, for the very first time since starting high school, I had forgotten to wait for Natalie. I felt so bad. *I have to call her straight away when I get home. Hope she doesn't think I will forget about her because of Brad.*

CHAPTER 9
Verona, Italy, March 2000

Last week I fell on the bus. I promise myself I will never fall again. I am working on my fitness and right now I weigh 53 kilos. Just three kilos to lose before I try chatting to Brad. He said he likes models. I checked the model agency weight/height standards, which follow the American chart; a model has to be 105 lbs and 5'6" tall. I'm counting my reduced calorie intake to help me lose weight fast. A model consumes about 1200 calories a day. Mom is working at grandfather's office so she is not home during lunch hour, I'm able to skip some meals. Some evenings she cooks just vegetables and a protein, which saves me from leaving my carbohydrates on the plate. At school snack time, I alternate between pieces of apple and five pieces of mini carrot. When I feel like treating myself I have a bar of Kinder Bueno. I drink about two liters of water a day. My skin certainly looks healthy and smooth on this new diet.

"I'm constipated," Susanna says to her mother as soon as she walks into the house.

"Are you sure?" Olga asks from the kitchen counter taking her eyes off the health magazine she is browsing.

"Of course, I'm eating too much carbohydrate and my chemistry teacher told us that too many carbs are bad for our digestive system," Susanna says the first thing that pops into her head.

"Well then, tomorrow after school, go pick up some laxatives. I'm going to help in grandfather's office so I won't be here. Buy me some of this while you're there." Olga hands her daughter a magazine cutting.

"Anti-cellulite cream, Mom?" Susanna looks at the model on the cover, she looks so young. "At what age can I use this kind of product?"

"When you don't have pimples." Her mother laughs but keeps her eyes on the magazine.

"I don't have pimples!" Susanna complains.

"Then wait until you're eighteen. Right now you are perfect as you are." Olga looks up from the magazine, smiles and tucks a tuft behind Susanna's left ear.

"Why doesn't Brad like me?" Susanna whispers a little too loud.

"Brad?"

"Nothing, nothing..."

"What is it, Susanna?" she closes the magazine "Since we've been back from Asiago, you and Natalie don't spend time together as much as you used to. And you run into your room minutes after meals..."

"I have so much schoolwork to do. As the doctor pointed out, I'm under a lot of stress. Don't worry, Mom, when school is over I'll be back to my normal self. I can't wait till summer." Susanna forces a smile for her mother.

"Good. But don't lose any more weight." Olga looks back down at the magazine.

After school the following day, Susanna doesn't wait for Natalie. Since mid-February she has stopped waiting for her best friend. Susanna thinks she can't talk to her friend anymore because she will ruin her healthy eating journey. *I think she was jealous of Brad and me, because she can't show off her boyfriend as I can.* Susanna walks to the pharmacy, buys her laxative, her mother's anti-cellulite cream and then after some thought she asks for cleansing salt. Next, she goes into the bakery shop nearby to buy a bottle of water. Outside she takes two laxatives.

After dinner, before her secret workout, she dissolves two tablespoons of cleansing salt in a big glass of water. It doesn't work as fast as the laxatives, but they do the trick. Susanna goes to bed satisfied with herself, but at two a.m. stomach cramps wake her up. She rushes into the bathroom. She returns to her room, but finds it difficult to close her eyes. *I could eat a whale! Think of something else, think of something else... I wish the unconsciousness of sleep would take me.* She looks at the alarm clock on the bedside table — 4:00 AM. Susanna starts to count sheep. Finally sleep veils her eyes as the morning rays begin to filter through her thick shutter blinds.

CHAPTER 10

The next morning, as she descends the stairs, the smell of freshly made French toast snakes up Susanna's nostrils like the odour of an old greased wall paper. Her stomach turns upside down. She ignores the nausea as she takes the glass of cold water and a slice of lemon she prepared the night before out of the fridge. In front of the stove Susanna's mother is busy cooking the toast. Susanna sits at the breakfast bar, sips her water. Behind the glass she squints her eyes as if looking through a crystal ball. She observes her mother, her hair, a messy top knot. A stubborn grey hair finds its way among the brown. Her skin coloured vest clashes with her flawless milky skin tone. Olga turns to her daughter. Her perfect oval face, even without make-up, smiles at Susanna. Only the wrinkles around the corners of her mouth giveaway her age. Olga leans her head to one side and starts to hum a tune her daughter doesn't recognise but that particular gesture plays a memory in Susanna's mind's eye.

It's Christmas morning, ten years earlier. Susanna, her sister and parents are in Ghana to celebrate Christmas with her paternal grandmother. That particular morning, Susanna tries rice pudding for the first time, her grandmother calls it *rice water*. After breakfast she sits at the kitchen table as her granny takes rice, tomatoes, seasoning maggi cubes, onions and a bottle of oil out of the cupboards. She puts everything in a plastic shopping basket. All this time she hums a tune Susanna doesn't recognise. She turns to Susanna and says, "All these are for Esi to cook our Christmas dinner with." The chocolate skin seems to melt into the white of the eyes as she smiles. Her granddaughter smiles back. "Now, you and I are going to prepare dessert." From the lower cupboard she brings out a big silver bowl.

"What are we going to make?" Susanna opens her hands like a butterfly.

"Chin chin–" her grandmother leans towards Susanna and touches the tip of her button nose with a finger, leaving a mark of flour.

"My favourite snack!" Susanna says. "Can you sing the chin chin song for me?"

"Of course." Grandmother nods her head and as she takes each ingredient out from the dispenser she sings, "To make chin chin we need..."

"Flour..." Susanna says a little too loud. Her grandmother scoops out some flour from a container.

"We need..." her grandmother carries on singing

"Butter..." Grandmother scoops some butter with a large spoon. "Nutmeg, pinch of salt..." Susanna takes grated nutmeg and smiles, her missing front tooth giving away her age.

"...And don't forget little bit of water. Mix until it turns into soft dough," Grandmother says in her turtle pace like tone. Once she thinks it looks good, she tells Susanna to roll out the dough with a rolling pin. Grandmother uses an empty green bottle to roll hers out. She hands a tiny plastic knife to Susanna who imitates her as she watches her granny cut the dough into small pieces.

"After we cut the dough into pieces, we will bake the chin chin, I like the taste better, instead of fried taste." She smiles. Susanna looks up her grandmother's beautiful chocolate face, candid white hair and broad perfect white smile.

As soon as the tray of tiny dough goes into the oven Susanna's grandmother calls out "Esi, Esi!" The house helper walks into the kitchen, her pale sole slapping the cold, smoothly-cemented floor. "You can start cooking Christmas dinner. Go fetch the chicken the driver brought the other day."

"Can I go with her, Granny?" Susanna pleads.

"You can go but don't disturb Esi with too much talking." Esi reaches her hand out. Susanna places her tiny soft hand into a big dry hand, a hand that tells the story of a hard working girl. Esi was the girl that helped Susanna's grandmother cook, wash, iron and clean the whole house. Still she has a smile for everyone in the house and the neighbours, as if she was born to please people.

Once outside, Susanna sits on a red dusted floor as Esi sharpens the knife on a sharpening stone. The chicken sits in its portable coop, unaware of its near future. A pot of water boils on a stove, made out of fine textured sand, red soil, water, dried grass, ash, sweet potato leaves and banana stems. When the water boils over, Esi scoops some in a metal cup and with her bare hand takes some to soften the throat of the chicken.

"Don't you burn?" Susanna asks shocked.

"Oh no, I'm used to it." Esi smiles revealing a set of not so perfect teeth.

"Why do you have to do that?" Susanna's inquisitive side doesn't allow Esi to work as fast as she would normally. She doesn't answer, so Susanna asks again "Why do you put hot water there – on its neck?"

"I want the chicken to feel the least pain possible."

Susanna rests her head on one hand, a part of her wants to be away from the scene. To see no blood. Another part wants to see how Esi kills the chicken. After Esi pulls a few soft feathers away from the bird's neck, Susanna asks "Why does it have to be a rooster?"

"Male chickens have more meat, they're greedy." Esi chuckles

"But I like it when it crows in the morning," Susanna says, a little bit sad.

Suddenly Esi is solemn, points the knife to the sky, whispers something in Twi – one of the many dialects in Ghana – then, in one smooth movement, she slits the throat of the bird. The bird spasms under Esi's feet for a while. Susanna puts her hands on her eyes. Then slowly parts her fingers to see the feathers of the bird has stopped moving. There is a patch of blood where its head has just been. Esi immerses the animal in the boiling water and then starts to pluck away the feathers. Susanna tucks her chin on her chest and looks on as Esi pulls feather upon feather away. At each pull, Susanna jumps up on the spot.

"Poor roaster. It looks so funny without feathers," she says as she reaches forward to look properly.

"Don't feel sorry for our dinner." Esi laughs

"I don't want to eat that." Susanna shakes her head.

"Are you sure?" Esi is still laughing

"Yep! It's too skinny without feathers." Susanna turns to look at a female chicken walking about, gracefully, with all its feathers.

For the evening party, Susanna wears a white dress with peach roses at the hem. Her mother pulls her hair into two pigtails. Once they're all pampered they gather near the Christmas tree in the living room to sing Twi Christmas songs. Susanna claps and looks up at everyone with glee in her eyes. When Linda sings, Susanna claps a bit louder to show everyone how proud she is of her talented sister.

After singing the songs, they sit down to eat. The smell of the freshly cooked chicken stew, oily rice to which Esi added onion and oily beef stock to make it yummier, fill the room. For dessert there is baked chin chin and vanilla ice cream.

Susanna wiggles on the chair when she sees all the delicious food. She smiles and claps her hands when her granny serves her first. She gives her the chicken thigh and liver, the part Susanna likes the most.

The vision of the killing and the blood on the ground doesn't stop her from asking for a second serving even before her plate is empty.

"Susanna... behave." Her mother looks disappointed as she continues "You're going to be fat if you keep on eating like that." Susanna licks her lips because she's having another mouthful of Esi's delicious rice and stew. She didn't care about getting fat.

"Susanna! Susanna?" Her mother's voice brings her back to the present. "You haven't touched your toast."

"Ehm?" Susanna looks with a frown.

"Your toast is getting cold." Susanna looks away from the plate. Her eyes fall on the clock above the fridge.

"Oh, but I'm running late... for the bus." Lying is so easy for her lately.

"Dad will drive you. At least take a piece of toast." Her mother's suggestion opens a void beneath her. *No way! This will not happen, you are not going to eat that toast. It will mean you are not behaving,* the voice tells her.

"I'll take the bus with Natalie..."

"Nonsense, your father is going to work early and he can drive you and Natalie to school" Olga waves her hand in the air as if fighting with a mosquito.

"Mmm, I haven't seen her in ages and I want to tell her something." Susanna's heart sits heavy in her chest. Her stomach is on a rollercoaster. "Really, I will eat my toast later. I'm running late."

"Your father will give you a ride. Nelson, take both Susanna and Natalie to school, would you?" Olga suggests, and Susanna hates her mother for that. She turns to look at her father, his milk chocolate skin tone is shiny thanks to the cocoa butter he uses.

"Sure." Her father puts the morning paper down, then devours his last piece of French toast. Susanna watches in agony. *Plan b, plan b... what shall I do?* She takes a little bite of the toast and chews, counting slowly. In the meantime her mother phones Natalie. The watch on the wall reads 7:40 A.M. In the end she decides to bite the toast in big pieces, she swallow without chewing.

"I have to get a notebook from upstairs." She runs up the stairs three steps at a time. Once in her bathroom, she throws up the toast while the thought *no more like a greedy rooster* clouds her mind. She weighs herself. 115 pounds! She rinses her mouth out with mouthwash and runs downstairs. Feeling light.

CHAPTER 11
Verona, Italy, October 1999

I had my first real date with Brad two Saturdays after we became boyfriend and girlfriend. We didn't go out before because Brad was always busy with hockey. For the first date, I wore a blue tank top covered with a blue and white stripy cardigan over a pair of white trousers. I left my hair loose, with a crystal pin clipped on one side and put on the sapphire stone earrings Linda had given me for my birthday. I thought I looked like Princess Jasmine.

I was still applying lip gloss when I heard Brad greeting my father downstairs. He was early, so I took my time putting together the finishing touches.

"Brad is here." My mother walked into my room. "How are you getting on?"

"I don't know what to do with my hair." I pulled my hair into my hands.

"Since when did my little girl become so interested in how her hair looks?" She patted my curls "You look beautiful no matter how you style your hair." She circled my shoulders with her arms.

"Yeah, right –" I hid a shy smile. "Mmmm, I think I'll leave it loose." I twisted my tufts into a bun and then left them falling on my shoulders. I looked at my mother through the mirror and smiled while a lump rose in my throat.

"Really, you are beautiful." She tightened her hug around

my shoulders. I loved my mother's company. It felt good to have that female bond between us. "He *is* cute."

"Mmmmmm, I know..." I bit my upper lip.

She smiled. "Where is he taking you?"

"Not sure."

"Wherever he takes you, I hope you enjoy your date." I thought she was about to cry, but she smiled and hugged me tighter. I forgot about my hair and hugged her back.

"Oh, Mom..." The words were about to choke in my throat, but I forced them out. "I'm so happy!"

"I am glad." She kissed my forehead. She followed me outside my room.

As I was descending the stairs, I heard my father's throaty laugh, then heard Brad say something about his father's involvement in the Second World War.

"Incredible," I heard my father say. "While my father went to Britain to fight for the war effort, your father was in Italy with the Canadian army. Well, well, *ragazzo,* we have something in common," my father said. From the conversation and the tone of his voice, I could tell he liked Brad. "Did your father ever consider returning to Canada?"

"Oh no, no. My mother would never go with him. And all our friends are here in Italy." Brad paused, then said, "I've been there on holidays though." He hesitated and then asked, "Susanna told me you are a banker... How did you become a banker?"

"Hard work boy. Hard work and studying hard. Nothing is given free in this world." My father paused for a second, then said, "I studied economics in Ghana, and then went back to the UK to complete my masters. It is there I met Olga, my wife. She was studying business like me." He smiled and then asked Brad "Do you want more coca-cola?"

"No *grazie, signor* Danso..." Brad was about to finish his sentence when I entered the room.

"Daddy? We're going out now."

"Okay, okay." My father looked so different from a few years before. I remember when Linda had told them about her boyfriend. Our dad had freaked out. At the time he'd said "You're too young."

Mom had defended Linda. "You once told me you fell in love when you were thirteen..."

"But that was a long time ago and I'm a boy."

Later on, I overheard her say, "It is normal to have *fidanzatini* at fifteen. Don't pull that face, Nelson. Giving freedom to the girls will make them responsible and they will be open about life issues... You know what I mean?"

So that evening I felt comfortable when I said "We won't be late." I hugged Dad first.

"I know, *amore*, have fun and take care." He hugged me and stamped my check with a kiss.

Then he continued, "Brad... ride safely."

"Yes, Sir."

"*Fatte i bravi.*" Both my parents said.

"Always." I smiled as I closed the door behind us.

"You look nice with your hair like that." Brad said, handing me the helmet.

"Thanks. You do too." He wore a red winter bomber jacket over a pair of dark loose jeans. His hair was flattened down with gel. I pushed my hair into the helmet and climbed onto his Vespa. Once he'd reassured himself that I was seated behind him, he took off fast, rising spectacularly on the back wheel. I was sure my parents' hearts skipped a beat at the sight.

Brad found a spot in the parking lot at near the Verona Arena amphitheater in Piazza Bra, the center of Verona. He helped me off the seat, then once he double-checked that his Vespa was not close to any old beat-up moto, he balanced the front wheel on the kickstand. While he was parking, I saw two guys from our school, staring at us. Once Brad had finished securing his scooter, he pulled me tightly to himself, forcing my head to rest on his chest. He smiled down at me. My heart was shooting inside like a crazy man with a gun. We walked like that past the Arena towards Via Mazzini, my mother's favourite shopping street. Every big designer had a boutique on Via Mazzini.

Brad was the first to break the silence.

"Are you still worried about us together?" He said looking down at me. I felt so little.

"No – but... I wonder why you like to make the other girls jealous when they see us together."

"You shouldn't worry, I really *like* you. But if you are uncomfortable with the attention I give you because of how the other girls feel – then you are welcome to call us off." He gazed at me with those deep honey-hazel eyes. I bit my lower lip. He curled down to kiss me. I could not hide my big smile any further. I was so excited I wanted to burst out of my skin, but I pulled out of the embrace and dragged him by the wrist towards the Louis Vuitton store.

"Nice bags." I smiled over my shoulder at him.

"Do you like designer clothes?" Brad asked, wrapping his arms around my waist.

"As my mother says, *one good piece of expensive clothing is better than a million cheap ones.*" I imitated my mother's voice. I looked squarely at him, but he didn't seem convinced. "Isn't the jacket you're wearing designer?"

"Yeah, but I bought it from a friend of mine, who got it from China." I looked over my shoulder. He was standing there now with his hands tucked into his pockets.

"Still, it's an expensive brand."

"I'm not as lucky as you to have an original. Most of my designer clothes are hand-me-downs from friends or cousins."

"Why am I lucky?"

"Your family owns practically half of Verona."

"Really?"

"Of course! I mean your grandfather is the biggest entrepreneur in Verona. Doesn't he have villas in the city and abroad?"

My heart was pounding. I felt awkward listening to Brad talking about my family assets. Nobody had ever put me in such a situation before and I didn't know how to react. I managed to say, "If you say so, maybe you are right... Mmmmm, thinking about it, I am so loaded I can buy you."

"Of course, I am right... ah, wait a sec, you can't buy me,

and it's your grandfather who is loaded, not you."

"Well, my grandfather loves me very much, so I can tell him to buy you for me."

He let out a laugh and walked away from the window. I watched him go. The late afternoon sun turned his light brown hair into gold. In that moment, confused feelings struggled inside. I wanted to go up to him and embrace his beauty, but another part of me wanted to go up behind him and slap his perfectly shaped head. He had just pressed the family button and I didn't like people pressing that.

I didn't like people making me feel guilty because my family could afford designer clothes. But most of all, the wealth Brad was talking about was mainly my grandparents', not my mother's or father's. Plus, my grandfather didn't own half of Verona, and he'd worked his ass off to get where he was. Nothing had been given to him on a silver platter like a prince. Plus, his wealth was not my business and I didn't want to talk about it, especially *not* on my first date.

On impulse, I went to grab Brad's arm and hugged him.

"You are right, the money is my grandfather's. Not mine or my mother's," I whispered. I didn't want to argue, but his tone told a different story.

"Yeah, right! You're both heiresses."

I was dumbfounded.

"Did you say your father was a soldier?" I said trying to change subject.

"Yep, a Canadian soldier. He fought in the Second World War. My mother was a factory worker, but both are retired. Now my father works in a nearby vineyard to fill his spare time." He looked at me as if he was challenging me.

"Nice. Have you ever tried working in the fields?"

"No, and I am not going to ask you the same question because I know the answer."

"And I will not contradict you, but I will say that my grandmother used to work in the fields after the Second World War to help support her family."

"I guess your father just has British citizenship." I felt as if I was under police investigation.

"No..." I considered what to tell him next. For a moment I thought about not telling him anymore, but then something made me say, "He is both British and Ghanaian, and he is very proud of his Ghanaian origins."

"Why doesn't he want Italian citizenship?"

"If you really want to know, you can ask him when you take me back."

"Sorry. Oh look at the time. The film is about to start. I will buy you an ice cream after the film. There is a lovely *gelateria* next to Giulietta's castle." The caring and bubbly Brad I loved re-appeared again. I let him circle my shoulders. I relaxed my head on his chest and forgot about the silly conversation we'd just had. He smiled down at me and gently stroked my cheek. My heart went back to settle in its proper place instead of rubbing at my throat.

Before we entered the cinema, he stopped me on the sidewalk. The next thing I remember was his soft lips on mine. I returned the kiss in the way I remembered from my teen magazines, but my hands shook on his shoulders. Inside my belly... oh, it wobbled like a house during an earthquake.

Brad was a master in the art of kissing. His soft lips played with mine, teasing them gently. The moment was so precious I wanted it to last forever. But a few seconds later, Brad moved away as if to assure himself that I was still under his spell. His gaze made me feel hot inside. The sidewalk was not the most romantic place nor the place I used to dream about having my first kiss. However, my daydreams never stretched as far as kissing Brad. While he was still looking deep into my eyes, I looked at his smooth *burro di cacao* moistened lips. At that moment, I adored his lips more than anything in the world. As he moved a falling curl from my face, he smiled. My heart started to beat an exotic drum in my chest. He caressed my hair and began to kiss me again. This time he introduced something warm and tender into my mouth and I felt a tingling sensation running down my spine. Then butterflies began to dance in my stomach. I felt electric shocks through my entire body. I asked myself *why do they call it French Kiss. They should rename it Electric Kiss.* The electricity took me flying over the Dolomites and back to the pavement of Via Mazzini in Verona city. I was about to go on another trip around the beautiful landscape of Veneto when a rude passer-by shouted, "Get a room!"

I peeled my chest off Brad's and rested my hand near his heart. I looked at him and giggled. He gifted me with one of his dimpled smiles as I encircled his neck with both my arms. I felt wonderful. He laughed and his arms tightened around my waist. Standing close to him made me aware of his height. I had to throw my head back to look into his eyes. I stood on the tip of my toes and gave him my own version of a French kiss.

The little display of affection on the pavement had broken the ice we created before with our conversation about my family. Once in the cinema, we chose seats near the back, away from the crowd. Instead of watching the movie, we had an important discussion to make with our lips. He leaned toward me, putting his fingers under my chin, forcing me to look him in the eyes. I pursed my lips and closed my eyes ready to receive his mouth, oblivious to the audience surrounding us. He gathered me into his arms, pressing his chest tightly against mine. My nipples tingled so I moved away a little. As I did so, he played with my hair, still embracing me with his other arm. I liked that. I liked the way he tickled my ears with his lips, the way his fingers played around my neck. I liked his teasing kiss-bites on my cheek throughout the film.

After the film we went to buy ice cream.

"What would you like?" Brad asked me.

"Vanilla and strawberry in big waffle cone."

"That's a lot for a late snack. No wonder you have plus size models bottom." he said laughing.

I didn't say nothing, just pulled a corner of my lower lip into my mouth. He circled my shoulders and said, "You know I'm just kidding right?"

"Okay." I hid a smile in his embrace.

We got our ice creams and walked hand in hand to his Vespa. Once we'd finished eating our *gelato,* he drove us to a hill near my house.

"Like this place?" Brad asked as he pointed to Verona piazza.

"Nice." I walked to the edge and sat on the grass, overlooking the panorama. "I love looking at Verona from here. Look at the Arena glowing like it's on fire. No, it's smiling. Do you think people come here to watch the music festival when it's in the piazza?"

"Maybe." Brad shrugged. I looked up into the starry sky. I returned my attention to the lights of the city, dancing in front of my eyes.

"Did you see any of the film?" Brad asked coming closer to me.

"Not really. You?" I smiled, hugging my knees and resting my chin on them.

"Yes..." He waited to see my reaction, which was predictably disappointing. I didn't do anything. So he said, "You were the lead female character and I was kissing you the whole time."

"Huh..." I glowed like Arena at night and my eyes crinkled in a smile. A gust of cold wind blew through the trees. I wrapped my arms together from the sudden chill.

"Are you cold?" He rubbed my arms through my coat. I couldn't resist the warmth of his body. I kissed him. I felt the heat spreading through me. I held his face between my hands and didn't let him go. He whispered, "Sometimes I wish I was in Canada."

"Why?" I was short of breath.

"I would have my own car instead of a motorbike."

"But if you were in Canada, we wouldn't be together kissing each other at the edge of the city of Verona in Italy." I ruffled my hands in his short hair.

"Mmmm," He stamped a kiss on my lips then said, "It's getting late."

"Yeah," I sighed, getting up onto my feet.

CHAPTER 12

The week before Halloween, I was sitting under the chestnut tree near the parking lot with Brad and some kids from Spanish class, when I saw Carla walking towards us. She was wearing a short, grey fur winter coat. Underneath, one could see a see-through tight white sweater, her bra was scarlet red. The tops of her boots were trimmed with real fur. As soon as the guys turned in her direction her walk shifted from normal to tiger strides. She was beaming. She sat next to me and pulled a card from her pocket. I carried on eating my Kinder Bueno.

"Su, smell this." She shoved the card under my nose before I had the chance to answer. "This is a handmade pumpkin-scented invitation card." She just kept on talking "My father's girlfriend has a friend from North America who does these special cards. Because you are one of my favourite friends –" or *do you mean one of the few who you manage to corner in order to blast out your nonsense?*

"I'm giving it to you before the party is announced to the crowd."

"But I heard about your party from Natalie, who is not even in our school." I wanted to bite my tongue but it was too late.

"Who told Natalie? I'm sure it was Licia. She's such a slut. She comes to clean the stairs of our house twice a week. She might have heard me talking to my dad." Carla rolled her eyes, then surprisingly bit a piece of my Kinder Bueno. I let out a sign and swallowed saliva to stop myself from saying something. She carried on, "I will tell my dad Licia listens to our conversations. She will end up losing those pennies she scrubs the stairs for."

She took a can of diet coke from her small bag. I felt bad for Licia – no matter who Natalie got the information from – this was going to cost her a job.

"You know I was kidding, right, when I said Natalie told me?"

"And I was kidding when I said that Licia gets paid very little — my father is too generous with her. She doesn't clean the place well enough to get all that money. My dad pays her as if she works full time... Thinking about it, I will not have my father sack her. I'll just make sure she doesn't get anything for what she does." She spoke quickly and gulped down her diet coke. I looked at her and wondered how bad her family situation was for her to be so bitter.

"Natalie didn't tell me anything. I was just teasing you." I held her gaze, but she didn't seem to care.

"*Amore*, Giulio!" She stood up from the bench and ran past me towards her boyfriend. I sat there with her pumpkin scented card clutched in my hand.

"Oh *Mrs Lawson*, this is an honour." Natalie said when she saw me waiting for her after school "I thought I was never going to see you again since the love story between you and Brad blossomed into... is it the fourth week?" She hugged me, smiling.

"Don't tease me! What about you and William? You're the one who's forgotten about me." I locked arms with her.

"Don't even go there. It's not going as smoothly as I would wish." She twitched her full lips.

"Is he mistreating you?"

She laughed, "William? No, he is amazing with me. The problem is my mom; she's getting suspicious and I'm finding it difficult to keep telling her lies."

"Why don't you tell her the truth? I'm sure she will be more understanding than you believe. I told my parents about Brad the other day and they were very understanding."

"Even your dad?" She asked, her eyes wide open.

"Even him! All he asked was 'Is he a responsible driver on his Vespa?'" I imitated my father's deep voice.

"What? I can't believe it." Natalie shook her head. "He's so different from my father. He is more... I don't know... European! Nothing like my traditional Ghanaian-minded parents. They think boyfriends and education can't mix. That's the kind of close-mindedness I have to deal with." She pulled out her lips. "Enough about me. Where is your Prince Charming? Did he take off on his Vespa without you?"

"I was tired of the usual royal treatment. I wanted to take the bus like 'you commoners'!" I squeezed Natalie's shoulders.

"Ah, so this is how you see me now – a commoner. Thank you very much. Wait till he lets you down. Don't come running to me."

"Oh, Natalie. You're not a commoner." I grabbed her waist and laid my head on her shoulder. "You're my best friend."

"Whatever."

"Now, seriously I wanted to talk about Carla." I let go of her waist.

"Why?" She looked at me, worried.

"Nothing important, just that today we were talking about her Halloween party and I mentioned I knew about it."

"Which is true."

"Right. But she's cross because she thinks Licia told you. She is going to ask her father to sack Licia or pay her less."

"That's so cruel of her."

"I'm so sorry. I should've kept my mouth shut."

"Don't worry. Licia has had enough of Carla's tantrums and she's going to quit anyway." Natalie patted my shoulder. "Licia won't allow that brat to walk all over her. I'm sure Carla was in a bad mood. Apparently her father has been arguing with her mother for the past month."

"Don't pass on that gossip," I said. Natalie shrugged. I carried on saying, "I'll race you to the bus-stop. Whoever gets there last is a rat!" Before I could finish the sentence I was running down the street.

CHAPTER 13

Halloween came and I didn't feel like going to Carla's party. I hated costume parties anyway, they reminded me of my pre-school days. One *Carnevale*, one of the teachers cut out a piece of yellow paper and put it around my head. When I asked her why, she told me my face was dark so I could be a sunflower. Back then I didn't get it, because all the other children had their faces painted with beautiful bright colours.

"What's wrong with you?" Brad asked me at break.

"I'm not well." Then I thought about it for a second, and blurted out, "I don't want to go to Carla's party."

"She's going to bite your head off."

"I know, I know... Don't remind me."

"Why don't you want to go?"

"I don't have a Halloween costume; in fact I've never celebrated Halloween."

"*No* way! Impossible! Which planet do you live on?" He was cracking up with laughter.

"Not on yours." I pulled my tongue at him.

"What do you normally do around this time of year?"

"Last year I went to Toscana with my parents and sister. What did you do?"

"I went to Fenice's Halloween party. Then on November first I went to the cemetery with my mother to honour my late grandpa."

"You still honour your dead relatives?" He didn't answer, so I continued. "The only person who goes to the cemetery is my grandmother..."

"What?" He said curtly.

"I was just – Sorry, I..."

"Doesn't matter." In that moment the end of recess bell rang. Brad took off and I had to run behind him. Once in class, he wrote a note and passed it to me.

I'm not cross. I was thinking about our costumes...I= Mark Antony... you...?

I filled up the rest of the space without much thought: *Cleopatra?* I passed the paper back to him. He read then looked at me with his dreamy eyes and dimpled smile. My heart skipped a beat. I turned back to the pages in front of me and ripped a piece of paper on which I scribbled: *GrandeMela shopping centre after school?* I passed it to Brad.

"Yes!" he whispered back to me.

"Brad Lawson, Susanna Danso, stop passing love notes to each other," Prof. Cazzanella shouted at us. The class roar with laughter. Brad turned red and I felt heat on my face.

After school he drove us on his vespa to GrandeMela shopping centre. Once inside the mall I went straight to the store where they sold Halloween costumes. Brad followed me as I flicked hangers aside looking for the right gold robe and ribbons. Thirty minutes later, I decided to wear one of my mother's eighties dresses instead. In the jewellery section

I found a gold arm cuff with the falcon detail on one end and a gold and white beaded headpiece the same little gold falcon head attached to the front.

"It's perfect," Brad said.

"I'll leave my curls loose and wear the headpiece on top," I said through the mirror.

"I can't wait until tonight," Brad whispered to me.

"Me too. I can't wait to see...Mark Antony." I gave him a peck on the cheek. I heard an old couple standing in the queue next to us say "They're so cute." I smiled back at them.

When we arrived at my house, Brad wouldn't stop kissing me and pulling me to himself.

"Can I come in?" he asked "Yes. Linda is not back until tomorrow. Do you want a sandwich?" I asked Brad as I took off my school bag.

"We surely can have a sandwich together," he said in a funny voice.

"You don't have hockey practice, do you?" I dropped his school bag next to mine and led him into the kitchen.

"I don't have any training for the rest of the weekend." He got hold of my waist and kissed me on the neck.

"Would you like something to drink?" I asked, going over to the fridge.

"Gin..." he said and I quickly turned to him. He raised his arms in the air and said, "I'm teasing you... Give me coca cola and ice. You take me seriously all the time."

"I was born serious, unlike you..." I smiled "Cheese and mortadella?"

"What?" He asked from the other side of the counter.

"Do you want cheese and mortadella in your sandwich?"

"Yep." He gulped coca cola.

We took our plates into the living room where I bit into my sandwich. After a long silence I said, "I could die for mortadella and cheese sandwiches."

"Didn't you tell me you could die for dessert as well..." he pointed out. I turned to watch him as he enjoyed his sandwich. He didn't look at me but said, "Mmmm, this sandwich is yummy, I like it... very nice."

After eating I took off my sweater and relaxed on the sofa next to Brad. He leaned into my shoulder. I looked at him, at his soft lips, wanting to kiss him, but I didn't make the first move. I loved his delicate touch on my face and his strong arms that protectively surrounded my waist. After too long for me, he rested his lips on mine. They tasted like caramel. He started to caress my neck. Then his hand moved further down... He fumbled with my bra under my long t-shirt.

"Hmmm... Brad..." I pulled away a little to look at him. "No... I'm not ready."

"When then?" He sat up away from me.

"I…, I..."

He got up "I better get going, it's getting late anyway."

"Brad, please?" a drop fell onto my cheek. I bit my nails.

"I'm not cross... It *is* getting late."

"Okay, I'll see you tonight?"

"Oh, sure..." He gave me a quick kiss on the cheek and left my house without looking back.

That evening my mother came into my room to give me the white dress I wanted to wear for the party.

"It's so soft and beautiful." I stroked the material as I sat on the edge of the bed, unsure about what to do. "Are you sure I can use it tonight? It's just a Halloween party."

"Of course, Susina" She kissed my forehead "You have to look good. It's just an old dress I don't wear anymore."

She helped me dress and put on my makeup. Once she'd finished, staring back at me from the mirror was an ancient Egyptian. My eyes looked bigger with the bold mascara and shadows my mother created with the black eye pencil and eye shadow. My cheeks were faintly blushed and my lips looked natural with a light peach gloss.

"Brad took me to the shopping centre to buy a few things." I showed her the headpiece while I put on the cuff.

"*Bellissima...*" She smiled at me through the mirror. I smiled back to mask my sadness.

My father drove me to the party when Brad didn't show up. He parked in front of Carla's house. As I made to leave the car the dress got caught between the seats. I was gently untangling it when I saw Brad parking his Vespa in front of us. I pulled the robe with all my force, but it wouldn't come out.

"*Uffa!*"

"What is wrong, Susanna?" Dad released the stuck hem.

"Nothinnnng!" I hissed. Brad was helping somebody off his vespa. I recognised her. It was the cheerleader captain, Gianna. She was dressed as a diner waitress in a mini dress that left little to the imagination. I quickly got out of the car to make sure that Brad saw me before going into the house.

"See you on Sunday," Dad shouted from the car.

"Okay." My eyes were locked on Brad. He was dressed as a cowboy. I was stunned but kept my cool as I slowly walked toward the house. When he saw me, he waved. I smiled, blood rushing to my head.

"Susanna, you know Gianna, don't you?" He said.

"Hey, Gianna." I said, but she walked past me as if I wasn't standing there. I knew she liked Brad and had been pursuing him since last year without luck. But, apparently, that evening Brad was suddenly getting closer to her. I couldn't understand him.

"Why her?"

"What do you mean?" He moved towards the door. I could tell he was annoyed with me from the way he kept closing his eyes as he spoke "She needed a lift and I was free so I gave her a ride."

"I thought you were coming to pick me up."

"Didn't you say your dad or mom was bringing you?"

"I didn't..." He opened the door and my words got lost in the loud music. The party was in full swing. People were dressed in all sort of costumes. I saw a Chinese dragon, a ghost and several police men.

As soon as we walked into the house, Gigi came over to us. *"Vu compra?* You wanna buy this?" he asked in a thick Italian accent, pretending to be a Senegalese street vendor. He wore a rasta wig and an African print t-shirt over a sweater. He had painted his face a tone darker. I stood there as he and Brad laughed. He had never been happy about me and Brad being together so I felt he was paying me back by being offensive and dressing as a Senegalese vendor.

I didn't dwell on it for too long. I saw Carla with Giulio who was dressed as a farmer.

More than anyone in the room, my attention was caught by Carla's costume. She wanted to be the queen of the night and she had succeeded.

"Hiya!" She said as she walked towards us "You look good, *Cleopatra*," Carla said teasingly.

"Look at you too, but tell me who are you dressed as?"

"Oh Susanna, so clueless! Isn't the theme of the party pumpkins! Of course I am Cinderella..." I curled my eyebrows in doubt. Her white mini dress with the puffy hem told a different story "Okay, I'm *sexy* Cinderella — the other one is so plain I wanted to upgrade her. Plus, my pumpkins will transform into a white sporty four wheels." She winked at me, smiling like I was her accomplice. Giulio came from the kitchen with a can of Pepsi for Carla. I could smell the alcohol in the drink, it was so strong. Giulio hugged her around the waist. He was so drunk it was possible that he might not have noticed me, as he started to play with the buttons of Carla's top. He then loudly whispered, "Cinderella, you turn me on."

Carla giggled. Heat spread onto my face as I turned to the other side.

The evening was getting very boring for me. Brad preferred spending time with Gigi rather than me. At one point I left him and went to talk to Ambra but missing him I went to search for him. As I walked about the house like a chicken affected by a disease, I saw the brim of Brad's hat under the stairs. I moved closer just in time to see him leaning into Gianna. My heart plummeted on the spot. I was so angry and upset my body felt numb. I stood there watching them. Ambra came to break the bad spell.

"Guys?"

Brad startled and his hat fell. Ambra hugged my shoulders and said, "Brad? What the hell?"

"None of your business," he said wiping the lipstick mark off his face.

"If you want to make your girlfriend jealous, do it with a better person than that."

I turned to look at Ambra, confused. I just wanted to get out of there.

"Are you feeling okay?" Ambra whispered to me. I turned to look at her, but couldn't see properly. I hated being humiliated in front of everyone. My heart was pumping violently against my chest.

"I want to go home." She walked with me past Brad and Gianna. He didn't look at me, but from what my mind registered, he did look embarrassed.

The following day I phoned Natalie to tell her what had happened the night before. She didn't say much, just agreed with everything I said. As soon as I put the phone down, Brad phoned me, I stood still as he whispered down the cordless and when he said, "I was out of my mind last night. You're beautiful, the only one I want." I knew I would forgive him like a drug addict wanting the next fix. I didn't mind the humiliation from the night before.

Few weeks after the hiccup in our love story, Brad invited me to his apartment, where he lived with his mother, father and sister. There were three bedrooms, an open kitchen and living room. On the walls were with pictures of forest and the Dolomite. His bathroom had the smallest bathtub I've ever seen. We were going to his room when I saw his sister walking out of her room. She was tall and bony. She wore a large brown jumper over loose jeans.

"Hey Kimberly, this is Susanna. She in my class."

"Hi." I waved my hand.

"Hello Susanna." She looked as if she had been sleeping. "See you later."

"Yep." I scratched behind my ear then tucked some curls.

Brad led me into his room. The space was occupied mainly by his single bed. The desk, with a small bookcase underneath, and a chair were facing a small window. On the walls were five posters of hockey players and a red and gold hockey stick.

Brad moved some books and clothes off his bed, sat down and pulled me next to him. He pointed at poster of a player wearing a green jersey with an *all-star* printed in capitals. "That's Mike Modano."

"Ah, okay."

"You don't know him so don't fake it."

"I'm not." I shook my head.

"Well, he's the all-time goal-scoring and points leader players in the National Hockey League." He stood up and took the stick off the wall. "Look here. He signed this for me couple of years ago when he was in Verona for a hockey event."

"That's really nice." I didn't know what else to say. He put the stick back. Instead of sitting next to me he leaned against the desk and melted me with his dimpled smile. "Why are you looking at me like that?" I asked.

"I love how sweet you're. I'm so sorry for my silly action two weeks ago."

"Apologise accepted."

"I understand if you want to wait, I really don't care about that."

"I like you and I don't want to ruin anything." I said. He moved closer to me. He cupped my face into his hands. I got up. We started kissing. He was so strong I fell onto his bed, lying flat with his weight on my chest, next thing I remember he was caressing my skin under my top.

This kind of scenes repeated for the rest of the month. We never went further than that. I let him feel my skin because he was so patient and respectful of me wanting to wait.

CHAPTER 14
Verona, Italy, December 1999

Finally the last day of class before Christmas break arrived. Everyone wanted to be out the door as fast as possible. Classes finished one hour early so Brad and I had lunch together in one of my favourite pizzerias in Verona center. At the restaurant, I ordered pizza *atomica*. It had spicy salamino, salsiccia, pineapple, anchovy filets, finely chopped red pepper and extra shredded mozzarella. Brad ordered rucola and cheese pizza, because he was still on his healthy diet as part of his hockey training.

"You know, you could try this diet with me." Brad offered without me asking for his help about my eating habits.

"Do I need to lose weight?"

"Not too much, just get a bit toned around the belly or the glutes."

"I feel fine with my weight." I lied "Shall we change topic."

"Okay by me. What time are you leaving for the mountain?" he asked me instead.

"Asiago?" I asked with my knife and fork down. I was eating with my fingers because it tasted yummier.

"Hmmmm." He chewed his piece.

"Monday morning. Tomorrow we'll buy all our gifts and do some last minute food shopping. Asiago is too expensive to shop for food." I bit into the pizza. Oil ran down my fingers. I licked it off.

"I thought your grandfather had enough money not to care about the pennies."

"Brad!" I frowned at him.

"Don't be so precious." He bit into his pizza, then continued, "If you have the money, just be happy to splash it around, no?"

I concentrated on the last piece of my pizza, saying nothing. After a while I asked, "When are you leaving?"

"Monday, not sure what time."

"Will you phone me?" I smiled at him.

"Give me your number." I found a piece of paper, wrote my Asiago phone number and put the piece of paper into his pocket.

Two days later, we drove up to my grandparents' chalet. Our family tradition was to get together on Christmas and Easter. Sometimes Aunt Marta – my model agent aunty – would turn up, I dreaded those times. She and my mother didn't get on very well. I always thought she wanted Linda and me to compete for our mother's affection as my grandmother had made her children do. She *always* picked on me, telling me how Linda knew which colours to wear to enhance her light olive skin tone. During family get-togethers, she took it upon herself to become my nutritionist. She would watch me eat as if I was a pig, while she picked at her food.

If I was unlucky enough to sit next to her, she would

whisper into my ear, "Look how healthy Linda looks. She is not eating all the food you're eating." Pointing her nose at my plate, she continued, "If you don't stop eating that big a portion, you will never lose the fat around your belly." She would then pinch my stomach. She made family time together a hell. *I wish this Christmas she'll be nice*, I thought as I finished unpacking.

Afterwards, I went downstairs while Linda rested. I was halfway down when Aunt Marta saw me. "Susanna, *piccola mia*, have you put on weight?" she said to me. I stopped in my tracks but she carried on. "Your sweater makes you look ill. Green does not suit your skin tone."

I shrugged, did a U-turn back to my bedroom in the attic. Being alone with her was the last thing I wanted. It felt like a siren wailing in the distance when she asked, "Where is your mother?"

"I'm not her babysitter," I answered without turning

"Susanna! How rude."

I went back to my room and stood on the terrace outside my window. All around were tall pine trees covered in thick snow. I sighed, exhaling cold vapour from my mouth. I tightened the multi-coloured blanket around my shoulders. The sun glittering in the background made it look like diamonds in the air. I stared out over the steep slopes, which looked like angels guarding the city. I loved going to my grandparents' chalet for the holidays, but I hated seeing Aunt Marta.

My mind went back to our drive up to Asiago. The winding streets were covered in snow and I was worried we wouldn't make it up to town. *Brad will be there*, I sang and danced in my mind. *This Christmas is going to be the best ever.* I smiled at the thought. Surrounded by such enchantment and thinking about Brad, my heart felt at peace.

CHAPTER 15
Verona, Italy, March 2000

Linda comes back to Verona for the Easter holiday but she is too interested in her music, university coursework and talking to Christian to notice Susanna's new behaviour. Susanna is able to do two sets of five hundred crunches without stopping. She does one set in the morning and another in the evening before bed. Her stomach is beginning to tone under her clothes. In her diary she writes:

22nd March,

The laxatives and the cleansing salt don't work as well as before. Two more kilos before my ideal weight, but it is proving more difficult than I thought. I don't know what else to do. I am going to the library to search for dieting tips. My thighs need toning, so I've added squats and side/inside leg kicks. I hope they help. This time I am eating because I don't want to faint.

One Sunday morning while Susanna is calculating her calorie intake at meals, she hears a knock on her bedroom door. When she answers, her father enters and sits at the edge of the bed. She looks at him but doesn't say a word. He speaks first. "How are you?"

"Fine." Susanna shrugs

"Good" He looks down at his shoes.

"Is everything okay?" Susanna looks away from her numbers.

"Mmmmm... No." He irons down the waves in the duvet cover with his left hand. "I don't know how to tell you."

"Tell me what?" Susanna bites off the skin of her nail.

"Granny Margaret. They just phoned me..."

Susanna lets out a sigh of relief.

"She's taken seriously ill."

"Oh?" is all Susanna says, just to say something, but all she cares about is the freedom with which she can lose the last few kilos. Her father mistakes her silence for sadness. He circles her shoulder in a hug, patting her hair to comfort her. She lets him hug her, while images of the foods she is not going to eat flip through her mind.

"Mom and I have to go to Ghana for some time."

"For how long"

"Don't worry, we're thinking a week while Linda is here to look after you. You will be fine, right?"

"Of course, I'll be fine. Linda is here…"

"We have to go first thing tomorrow morning."

Hurray, no breakfast. "Okay." Her mind is filled with her meal plans: *for lunch I will have a big glass of water, two rice cakes topped with soft cheese... Mmm, maybe not the cheese — too fattening. Cucumber, yes, cucumber is a healthy option.*

"Also, Aunt Marta is going to be in Verona. If you need anything, she'll be there for you."

"Aunt Marta?" Susanna looks up.

"Yes." He shakes his head then continues. "I know you

two don't get on, but it'll just be for one week."

"Don't worry, Daddy, I'll be fine." *I can check out how much a model should weigh these days.*

He tightens his arm around her shoulders.

The following day, Easter Monday, as soon as she wakes up, Susanna weighs herself: 51.5 kilos. After brushing her teeth, she joins her family downstairs. She feels light and happy. Her constant headache doesn't even bother her anymore. The sky is dark. The dawn light timidly peeks from behind the clouds. Susanna looks at the light with a sense of hope. *Brad will have me back again after this mega diet plan.* She smiles at the thought.

One Saturday afternoon, while Linda is playing the piano in the living room, Susanna says, "I'm off to the library."

"Okay. Doing anything after that?"

"No."

"Do you want to go shopping?" Linda looks away from the piano and smiles at her sister.

"If you want..." Susanna shrugs.

"Great, I need a few new things."

"We can meet around five, near the music shop."

"I see you're studying a lot these days."

"Hmmm, yeah." Susanna shrugs again. "See you later."

She walks up the path to the library entrance. She wonders who comes to the library on a nice Saturday afternoon, instead of shopping till she drops and drinking coffee in one of the smart cafés with friends. Once inside, she goes straight to the health section. She picks a few promising books, then she goes to the magazine section. The March issue of *Benessere* with a subtitle *Like Yourself and Be Happy* beams up at her. The cover shows a model holding a scale and biting an apple. She looks like the classic Carla type: flat tummy, toned legs, small breasts and impossibly beautiful. Susanna sits on the floor under the romance books and browses through her selections.

"Excuse me?" A young man pushing a library cart through the aisle calls her attention. "You're blocking the way."

Susanna puts everything in her handbag without looking at him and goes to check out the items. Outside, she finds a seat under a shaded tree. Now and again she glances at her watch. She is absorbed in the pages, enjoying the shady spot when the sound of a scooter draws her attention. The sound makes her think of Brad.

She hopes it is him, yet the negative part of her wonders what Brad would be doing in the library on such a lovely Saturday afternoon. Footsteps on the gravel path get closer but she keeps her head down. She smells a strong male aftershave, a familiar rainforest smell.

Lately her sense of smell is so acute it makes her crazy, especially when food is concerned. *Focus!* she tells herself, and she keeps the corner of one eye looking at the ground to see who is coming. She sees the thick boots of a slowly walking man, and walking along beside them she sees a pair of trainers. She looks up.

It *is* Brad, together with his father.

"Hi," Susanna says. The rays of sun filtering through the trees play in his hair. *How cute is he? Oh, Brad!* He nods back. She can't keep her eyes off his perfectly shaped face and honey coloured eyes.

"My father recognised you," Brad breaks the spell.

"Ah..." *At least his father is kind enough to remember you*, the voice in Susanna says. After few seconds, she turns to Brad's dad. "How do you do, Mr. Lawson?"

"Very well, as you can see. Haven't seen you in a while. Everything all right with you?"

"Yeah..." Susanna plays with her curl near the right cheek..

"Good, good." Mr. Lawson looks up in the sky and points his walking stick to the trees "Everything is changing."

"Must be." Susanna bites her lower lip and runs her hand through her hair.

"Reading anything good?" Mr. Lawson bends over to look at the title of the magazine.

"Oh, I'm just..." Susanna forces a smile. It's too late to close the page of the magazine. Her eyes fall on Brad, but he is looking at his trainers.

"*How To Be Skinny in Three Weeks.* Why are you reading an article like that?" Mr. Lawson closes his eyes and shakes his head "Do you want to lose weight? You are already so perfect!" He smiles and nudges Brad. Susanna looks, her cheeks hot. After a pause Mr. Lawson carries on. "Don't ruin yourself with bad habits like many girls are doing these days. My little daughter is very ill..." He looks at Brad and stops.

An awkward silence follows, which Susanna breaks.

"But I'm not... I'm not..." She hesitates then says "Hmm, Mr. Lawson, I have... to meet my sister." She gathers her books and magazines.

"Sure, nice seeing you. Come visit when you can." Mr. Lawson says. Susanna gazes at Brad debating *Do I ignore him or should I be polite. How would Carla behave?*

"See you at school, Brad." His name is bitter-sweet in her mouth. He nods without looking at her.

Susanna walks away, a flame of hope burning in her heart. But soon enough she's back in the vortex of doubt. *If I lose the last kilos I'll win back Brad. That's all I want! That's all there is! His father said I don't need to lose more weight because he's supposed to say that. But I saw the truth in his eyes. Brad's sister is small and pretty, so how come his dad said I don't need to lose weight? I feel like... oh my god I want to throw up. Dio mio, I don't know where to hide myself.*

"What's wrong?" Linda asks when she sees Susanna with her cheeks wet. She pats her sister's shoulders.

"Nothing..." Susanna hesitates then after a minute's thought, Susanna says "I just saw Brad and his father."

"Why are you crying then?"

"It doesn't matter." Susanna looks at Linda. A part of her would like to confide in her sister but the other part knows that Linda won't understand, she doesn't have my problem. She's beautiful and confident, every guy wants to date her. Susanna curls up her shoulders and follows Linda halfheartedly into the Fiorucci shop.

Inside Linda tries on half the shop. After nearly an hour, Linda declares, "I love these jeans." She pirouettes in front of the mirror. Susanna looks at the Lycra blue jeans Linda is wearing. "These kind are blowing Milan's models' heads away. This colour is so popular."

"Milan is Milan, isn't it?" Susanna says and rubs her eyes. "I'm so tired."

"What do you mean?" Linda looks at her sister through the big mirror.

"What?"

"What do you mean *Milan is Milan*. Can't I wear these?"

"I mean fashion in Milan is not popular here." Susanna shrugs.

"What's your problem?" Linda says a little angry "Why are you giving me that attitude? I know you don't care about fashion, but I don't believe these jeans are not popular in Verona either." Linda holds up her *Blondie* t-shirt with one hand, making Deborah Harry's scarlet lips twist into a grimace. Susanna notices Linda's flat stomach and wonders when her sister got so toned. She has always had a beautiful body, near to perfect, but her stomach was enviable right then. Susanna decides to increase her daily crunches up to two thousand five hundred.

"I'm just saying." She shrugs. "I must say they do look good on you."

"Do you want to try a pair?" Linda smiles and goes back into the changing room.

"Nooo, thanks... They'll look horrible on me."

"What?!" Linda winks at sister through the mirror. "Are you scared to show off those lovely skinny buttocks?"

"Don't tease me." Susanna's head feels light; the sensation makes her feel alive.

"Look, Su, you don't have to go through all that shit for a guy." A knot tightens in Susanna's throat. She wishes Linda wouldn't say anything, instead her sister continues, "Being good-looking is not everything a girl must strive for in this world..."

You can speak because you have the looks and talent. What do I have?

Linda carries on. "You are so beautiful you don't comprehend the power of your own beauty."

"Enough of the poetic speech, I'm not doing anything for a guy."

"Don't lie to me. I know when you're telling stories. Brad doesn't deserve you." Linda's words open up the tears Susanna has bottled up for too long. She wants to believe Linda, but all her heart and soul wants are Brad's kisses and arms wrapped around her. *I miss him so much, I miss the way he played with my curls, the way his kisses electrified me. I miss his naked body on my stomach. Linda, you don't get it. I am the one who doesn't deserve him.* Susanna would like to shout this to her sister but doesn't say a thing, instead tears stream down her cheeks.

"Hey... don't cry on me now!" Linda cups Susanna's face in her hands but she can't stop her sister's sobs.

"Are you girls okay?" A male shop assistant, wearing a pair of tight jeans and a low-cut V-neck top, approaches.

"We love these jeans so much they bring happy tears,"

Linda says theatrically. Susanna hiccups and sniffs again, wiping her eyes, which now make her look like a bloodshot vampire in the mirror. She looks down at the cream sofa to avoid eye contact.

Once out of the store, Linda, who looks as if she has just robbed the boutique, suggests a milkshake. An offer Susanna can't refuse because her sister looks so happy.

When they come out of the ice cream shop, the first person Susanna sees is Brad. He stops in front of the pet shop next to Romeo and Juliet's castle to point out something to the girl with him. Susanna recognises Brad's sister. She is wearing a light spring trench coat. Though she is just thirteen, her face looks older than her age. Her skin is stretched tightly against her bones. She looks so fragile and pure. Susanna envies her because Brad looks at his sister with such affection. Susanna feels horrible with the milkshake in her hand. She thinks about the toast she ate for breakfast. She sips the drink but all she can think of is the moment she can hug the toilet seat.

CHAPTER 16
Verona, Italy, April 2000

Two weeks since my parents flew to Ghana to see granny Margaret. I've managed to lose all the weight I needed to lose and for good measure I've lost few extra. I don't allow bad food (carbs and fat) to enter my stomach anymore. I eat lean protein and vegetables. Some days I consume only 300 cals. To be able to do that I have two big glasses of water in the morning, one small egg for lunch, green salad and five almond nuts. I eat in front of Linda — I don't want her to spy on me.

I don't know why but I can't stand Natalie right now and am avoiding her. She is calling the house non-stop. I know I haven't talked to her in ages, but I just don't want to. Last time she phoned, I didn't answer. Linda talked to her and later she told me that Natalie urgently needs to talk to me, but I don't feel like talking to her. I still wear my big sweaters and loose jeans. They keep my body safe and warm.

Brad is constantly on my mind, I can't even concentrate at school. Sometimes it feels as if I'm losing my mind.

After her diary update, Susanna goes downstairs. At that

moment the phones rings. Linda is nowhere to be seen, so Susanna answers the phone.

"Susanna? It's me, Nat." Her friend is the first to break the ice

"I know."

"How are you doing?"

"Fine. Why are you asking?"

"Hey, we haven't seen each in ages and I just want to know how my *best* friend is doing."

"Sorry... I'm fine... It's just... never mind."

"Are you really okay?"

"Yeah... How about you?"

"I'm putting on weight and I don't even know the reason."

"How is William?" Susanna asks to avoid talking about weight.

"Fine. What are you doing tonight?"

"Nothing important."

"Would you like to go for a pizza?"

Susanna is on the edge of declining, but the words that come out of her mouth surprise her. "Sure, I miss you." But guilt blocks her stomach too.

That evening Susanna joins Natalie at their local *bruschetteria,* the same place she went to have the pizza with Brad the last day of school four months ago.

Susanna hugs Natalie. They haven't seen each other since the beginning of the year and the first thing she notices about her friend is how her jeans are pinching around the waist.

"I'm not feeling very well these days." Natalie says out of the blue. "It's been a long time since we last spoke."

"Mmmm...."

"I miss you so much. Have I done something to make you stop talking to me?"

"No, no." Susanna heart tightens in her chest. "I miss you too, but school is getting so busy."

"I have my finals too, remember? I would never let that interfere with our friendship. All I ask is one hour of your precious time."

Susanna doesn't say anything but focuses on the menu. She takes her time to browse the menu. *I can opt for salad without the dressing, without the cheese or the croutons or I can be brave and refuse everything. I shouldn't be scared to refuse to eat in front of her. In fact that will show my control. Unlike her, I can be in control of what I am putting inside my stomach.*

Natalie is the first to order: salamino bruschetta and Caesar salad.

"There's nothing I fancy. I'd like a glass of lemon iced tea." Susanna says as she pushes the menu to the side.

"Are you sure you don't want a bite?" Natalie asks her when the pizza arrives.

"I'm sure!" *This is like the hundredth time she's asking you, she's judging you.* The voice snaps inside her.

"It's yummy." she says, all excited.

Susanna rolls her eyes behind her glass of lemon iced tea, but after a sip she says, "It smells delish, but I ate a bowl of pasta with Linda... You eat. I feel like exploding with this iced tea." She watches Natalie as she bites into the piecc with eyes closed.

"I love this place. William and I have been coming here often. That must be why I'm putting on weight." Natalie laughs, but it's not her hearty one. *Glad I'm not overfeeding myself then.*

"Your parents are letting you go out in the evening a lot?" Susanna asks to make conversation

"My mom is home most evenings, she lost her job. She doesn't mind me going out. Do you remember, she likes to know I'm going out with you."

"You didn't tell me that your mother lost her job." Susanna is surprised at the news.

Natalie's eyes open wide. "Are you kidding me? I've been trying to catch up with you since January, since you came back from Asiago. You never answer or return my phone calls. I don't even know what happened." She sips her coke. "You've been avoiding me. If it wasn't for your mom, I wouldn't know you and Brad broke up during the Christmas holidays." Susanna looks at the melting ice in her drink. Natalie carries on, "Don't worry, everything will be fine. I can only imagine the pain you are going through right now. But don't starve yourself for a guy."

"This is exactly the reason I didn't tell you. You are so judgmental, just like the rest of my family. I'm not starving myself. I eat all the time. Anyways, what do you know about being dumped? I'm fine!"

"I don't want to judge in any way. I love you very much and because I haven't seen you in ages I can tell you've lost some weight. That's all." Natalie wipes her mouth with the folded paper napkin. She smiles. One unusual thing Susanna notices about her friend is the ease with which she smiles, as if she is carrying a secret.

"I lost my appetite due to stress and schoolwork. But I'm fine," Susanna says a little bit calmer.

"Of course. Are you happy to be here tonight?" Natalie asks with her mouth full.

"Why are you asking that?" Natalie is getting on Susanna's nerves.

"Because I miss you and I want you to have fun."

"I'm okay... All right?" Susanna bites the skin off her thumb. It begins to bleed. "I need to go to the washroom, excuse me." Once in the washroom she goes and stands in front of the mirror to look at her face. What she sees is a chubby girl but the mirror reflects a girl with deep set eyes and collarbones sticking out of her sweater. She washes the blood off her hands.

Susanna wishes she could like that girl staring back at her, but all she really wants is the girl in the mirror to get out of her body. It's her fault she's not enjoying the *bruschetta* like Natalie. *It's your fault I'm here throwing up food. It's your fault that I'm losing myself.* But another strong voice shuts her up. *Stop talking nonsense. You need to thank me for achieving your goal. It's thanks to my determination that Brad will look at you again.* She washes away her tears, puts more pressed powder on and goes back to Natalie empty stomach.

CHAPTER 17

The next morning she wakes up and before she can form any thought in her mind she weighs herself. As if by magic, the scale reads 47 kilos. She feels triumphant, but her stomach wants to eat something to celebrate. She feels like treating herself with a "non safe" meal. She goes to the kitchen and prepares herself toasted bread with butter. She eats before drinking water. She regrets it for the rest of the day. After avoiding carbs for so long, her stomach was not ready to eat bread. Each time she drinks water she has to run to the bathroom. Luckily, by the time Linda takes her to go get her pedi-mani done, Susanna is feeling better.

On the way back Linda, insists on buying a doughnut. Susanna doesn't make a scene; she eats everything. But, as soon as they walk into the house, she runs upstairs straight into her bathroom. Short of breath, she goes first to the scale. It reads 48 kilos. The number is like a monster wanting to eat her. Hands shaking, she goes to the sink to wet her face with cold water, then kneels down in front of the toilet. With urgent hands she presses her stomach. Nothing happens. She punches her stomach but the pain is too much to bear. Her eyes are watering, burning. Her head is spinning. She goes into her room for the laxatives. She takes five pills and drinks them down with a diuretic liquid. *You are taking control, Susanna. Soon you will have Brad's affection. Just lose the last extra kilo.* Those are the thoughts that encourage her.

She goes back into the bathroom to do her sit ups.

Meanwhile, downstairs, Linda goes through the kitchen cupboards. Susanna hears her sister shouting, "I'm ordering pizza. What kind do you want?"

Susanna is on her five hundred and seventy-fifth crunch. *Can't lose focus now.*

"Margherita...with...extra...mozzarella." She forces out while mentally counting *five hundred and seventy-eight.*

"What are you doing?" Linda asks.

"Just... on the toilet."

"OK. I'll go and pick up the pizzas," Linda says.

Susanna's body gives up at the count of five hundred and ninety-six. She is out of breath but her stomach starts to rumble. She goes to sit on the toilet, but it is painful getting anything out. Panic overcomes her. She punches her stomach hard. In the end she tries to purge again. She drinks water from the sink and forces herself to bring out whatever was bothering her stomach. She kneels by the toilet for what seems like forever. She doesn't hear Linda coming home with the pizzas. Linda calls Susanna several times, but she doesn't hear her sister's voice. Linda runs to Susanna's room, where she finds her, unconscious, on the marble floor.

CHAPTER 18
Asiago, Italy, December 1999

The following day, Linda drove me to the ice rink. When we turned the corner, I saw Brad leaning against the wall, whistling. I smiled at the scene because I'd never seen my boyfriend with such a laid-back attitude. While at school, he had to keep up appearances and always looked cool.

"Have you been here long?" I asked as I locked my arm with his.

"Couple of minutes." He brushed his lips on my cheek and started to walk.

"What did you do last night? I phoned you." I looked up at him.

"I was watching a hockey game with my friends."

"Hockey at Asiago?"

"Yes, it's quite famous these days. The championship games happen every December, when tourism picks up."

"It's a good game, eh?"

"I like it. Most of my friends do too."

Asiago was such a beautiful place full of pleasant memories dear to my heart. *I am happy to make new ones with Brad.* We walked past the handmade wooden toyshop. In that moment I remembered a toy my grandfather had bought me years before. I smiled at the thought.

"Why are you smiling?" Brad asked me.

"I thought about a toy my grandfather bought me eleven

Christmases ago. I was so little and this shop looked huge." I laughed as another image appeared in my mind's eye "I felt like a *gnomo* when my parents or grandparents brought me here to choose my Christmas gift." We peered in the window, the light inside appeared dim compared to what my five-year old mind remembered from a long time ago.

"What was it?"

"It was a rainbow Russian doll. It was so beautiful I took it to Ghana with me, when I went to visit my granny that year."

"Ghana?"

"Yeah, it's one of the countries on West African coast."

"I know." He run his fingers through his short hair. "Do you always choose your own Christmas gifts?"

"Not always, I'm allowed to buy something I really like before *Babbo Natale* brings his through our chimney. What about you?"

"I never believed in Father Christmas." He kicked the snow covered street. "What about you? When did you stop believing in the fat white man with the big white beard?" He smiled, but I was quiet. "What did I say wrong?"

"Nothing..."

"Don't worry if you don't want to tell me." His dimples appeared as he smiled. "What do you think about a cup of hot chocolate?"

"Uh, I know the perfect place. Just down Via Ungaretti... Have you ever been to Filastrocca?"

"Isn't that place they make those dessert that are so delicate and fluffy?"

"Their hot chocolate drinks are to die for." I squeezed Brad's arm. Couples and happy families walked by us with Christmas shopping bags in hand. Parents were smiling at their little ones. I rested my head on Brad's shoulder. For the first time during the Christmas holiday I didn't feel lonely. I closed my eyes to allow the happiness to wash over me.

At Filastrocca I ordered *tiramisú*. It was fluffy like the snow outside and it lifted my soul. I offered him half but he had two spoonful.

"I can't eat too much. I have a game the day after Saint Stephen." Brad smiled at me.

"The day after Christmas?" He nodded and pressed his lips together. "I don't envy you. I love desserts and I can't see myself giving them up for anyone in this world."

Halfway through the cake, Aunt Marta's little voice in my head started to nag — *you are going to be fat this Christmas*. I took another mouthful and her voice faded out of my head.

Christmas came and went without much ceremony, apart from Aunt Marta criticising Prima, the cook, for preparing fried potatoes and grilled sausages. I turned a deaf ear to her comments. After dinner, I met with Brad. I gave him a red and blue Giorgio Armani scarf as a Christmas gift. He leaned forward to kiss me.

"Thank you very much, Susanna." He turned the scarf in his hands. "I didn't get you anything."

"I saw it, thought of you and bought it. I didn't expect anything in return." I pulled my hair to one side. *All I want for Christmas is you*, I sang in my head. Being in his company so much during the holidays was already making me giddy.

"I promise, when we're back in Verona, I'll give you something... unless... you want something right now." He pulled me under his armpit and gave me another kiss.

I jokingly slapped his arm. "Don't think things like that."

"What was I thinking?" he opened his eyes wide.

"Nothing." I lowered my head a little.

He rubbed his eyes. "I'm tired, but super-excited for the hockey game tomorrow. You're coming, right?" I'd completely forgotten about the game until he mentioned it.

"Oh, sure, I'll be there."

"I'll introduce you to my friends. We're going to have fun." We started to walk back to his scooter. He was so excited he couldn't see how nervous I became after he mentioned his *friends*.

CHAPTER 19

The day of the game, Brad was playing at seven in the evening. I took all day getting ready. My room was an ocean of jeans, sweaters, tops, skirts and shoes scattered all over the floor. After hours looking and turning my bedroom floor into a landfill, whilst kicking myself, I went to ask Aunt Marta to help me choose an outfit because Linda was out with no other than Christian, her ex. They'd been dating again since shortly after Halloween.

Aunt Marta found a pair of electric blue skinny trousers and a white sweater dress which were among my old clothes. Although it was cold and snowy outside, she told me to wear a pair of flat Gucci shoes she'd bought me as a Christmas gift. A fire lit inside me when she convinced my parents to let me straighten my hair.

After two hours of straightening and brushing, she pulled my hair into a half chiffon, making sure that the rest of my hair fell softly on the left shoulder. She applied mascara on my eyelashes. As a finishing touch, she told me to pout as she applied deep peach lip-gloss. After the makeover, I looked at myself in the mirror and nearly fainted because the girl staring back at me looked like an actress ready for the red carpert.

"Thank you, *Zia*," I said timidly. "I love what you have done."

"You're welcome... You're going to steal hearts!" She

smiled and patted my shoulder. I gave her a kiss on the cheek. She folded her arms across her chest, pleased with herself. The pride on her face brought the image of Brad and his friends to my mind. I was so eager to impress them. If Aunt Marta's last words were a premonition then, *I was going to steal hearts.*

Mom drove me to the stadium.

"You're so pretty," she said at one point on our way.

"Thanks, Mom." My face and ears were still burning from the fuss my family had made about my looks. But still, that evening I was happy to hear compliments. I wanted to look pretty standing next to Brad. Knowing some of his friends from school, I could tell the-out-of-school friends were going to be even more stuck-up.

"You remind me of myself when I started dating your dad when we were living in London." She looked at the street while she spoke. I glanced at her profile and saw her smile. I'd heard about my mother and father's love story many times before, but I didn't understand what I reminded her "How is that?"

"Oh, just the way you look... so much in love and all." She looked at me for a second. I turned my eyes back to the road, not wanting her to read my mind through my eyes. The car stopped at a traffic light. I looked at the red light which took too long to turn back to green. The journalist on the radio began to read the headlines of seven o'clock news, but all I could think was: *The game has started...* I began shifting in my seat.

"Did you hear?" Mom asked me as the light was turning green. "It's going to snow."

"What?" I turned to her, confused.

"The newsreader just said tonight there'll be a snow storm. Do you think you'll need a ride home? I can pick you up earlier."

"Huh...., but Brad's friend will bring me home," I was hoping to sleep at the *baita,* the youth chalet Brad was staying with his friends. I held my handbag tightly in my lap. I made a mental stock *toothbrush, deodorant, hairbrush, underwear, lip gloss...*! I wanted to share the room with Brad. Since the day he'd told me about the game, I'd been daydreaming about our warm bodies entangled together on a single bed. I was convinced Brad wanted me to sleep over after the game. I curled my hand over my lips, pretending to cough, in order to hide my smile.

"Are you sure? Daddy can come pick you up." She reached over the steering wheel to wipe the inside windshield with her hand. "Defo!" I didn't want my parents to spoil my romantic night with my boyfriend.

"Defo? What does that mean?" she turned to me.

"Definitely."

"Speak properly," she said. "Anyways, the roads are dangerous. I want you to be safe."

"I'm sure Brad will never put our lives in the hands of a crazy driver, I trust him."

"Okay, then. Have fun tonight. I hope Brad's team wins the game." She parked between two cars in front of the

THEODORA O. AGYEMAN-ANANE

stadium. I unbuckled my seat-belt and slid across the seat to kiss and hug her. I got out of the car before she could say anything else.

As I walked away over the snow-covered cobblestones, I could feel Mom's loving eyes on my shoulders. I straightened my posture, but I didn't turn. Before the entrance of the stadium could swallow my figure, I heard the wheels of her car skid on the spot, back out and drive off. I sighed and began to relax, but my insides were still roiling. A big part of me wanted to run after my mother's car, but the knowledge that Brad was waiting for me inside the stadium kept me moving.

CHAPTER 20
Verona, Italy, April 2000

When Susanna's parents return from Ghana, in front of their eyes they see a prisoner from a Nazi concentration camp, not their daughter Susanna. Linda tells them what has happened in their absence.

"*Snitch!*" Susanna whispers to her sister, enraged.

"Susanna? You promised, you promised to eat properly while we were gone. Instead you are skinnier," her father says crossly.

"I *have* been eating. Linda is lying." She looks at Linda, who is leaning against the wall near the living room door. "Didn't I eat most meals with you? Didn't I drink that big milkshake with you?"

"You did, but, well ..."

"What?" Susanna says curtly "I'm getting skinny because of my age, and the stress from school. I have my finals this year if you don't *remember.*"

"You need to eat more Susanna. The doctor said you should be careful of your diet." Her father seems annoyed, but Susanna thinks that she must fight for what she believes is her right as a human being.

"You must eat well," her mother chips in. "People in Africa are dying for lack of food —"

"They can have mine if they want." Susanna cuts short her mother's speech. "What does a lecture on starving children in Africa have to do with me? Are granny Margaret and our family members in Ghana dying for lack of food? I feel great and you can't do anything because my body is my own." Every eye in the room is looking at her, but they don't say anything. That evening, in revenge, Susanna doesn't touch her plate.

At dinner the following day Olga says, "We think you should see a dietician if you want to lose some weight." She looks at Nelson. Susanna thinks their suggestion is *intriguing*, but soon she reads anger in her father's eyes which is not intriguing at all. Olga continues. "We think it will be better than the yo-yo dieting those magazines tend to promote."

The voice in her mind rings the alarm. *Careful, Susanna, this is a trap. If you go to the dietician they will never allow you to eat three hundred calories or less a day.*

When she realises this, she wants to kill them, but checking her tongue, she says "But I don't want to lose weight, so I don't need a dietician."

Her father is the first to put his fork down. "Susanna, we gave you too many chances to be healthy by yourself. Now, you must listen to us."

"I'm sixteen and I know what's good for me. I said I don't want to go anywhere! I'm fine!" To prove her point, she takes a mouthful of her lasagna. They both look at her, unconvinced.

The following day at school, Susanna thinks that Brad is looking at her a lot. She thinks it's an invitation, so she asks Melanie to swap seats. Since they broke up, he's been sitting next to Melanie, "the witch".

"How are you doing?" Susanna asks, even though Brad seems focused on his French book.

"Are you talking to me?" Brad turns left and right pretending not to see Susanna.

"Yes..."

"What do you want?" He raises his voice.

"Shhhh!" Susanna can feel her heart beating violently against her chest. "No need to shout!"

"I don't want to talk to you!"

"You said... you said if I lost weight, we would get back together." The words are very faint and even as she utters them she notices how silly they sound. Her throat is tight.

"When did I tell you that? I never told you to lose weight."

"But you said..."

"In which language do you want me to tell you? You're not my type!"

"Why did you ask me out then? Why are you looking at me now?" This time it was Susanna who is raising her voice.

"Do you want an answer?"

"I guess your type is Gianna or Carla?"

"If that makes you happy." He shrugs

"Tell me the truth."

"What's your problem? OK, will the truth keep you away from me?"

"Just tell me..." Susanna spits out the words.

"*Silenzio!*" Prof. Cazzanella clears his throat.

"Gosh... you were a bet and I won. Are you happy? Now, leave me alone. And by the way, you look like a ghost."

Susanna gets up from the desk. Prof. Cazzanella sees her coming towards his desk

"Yes, Susanna?"

"Can I go to the bathroom?"

"We just got back from break. Why do you want to go out again?"

"It's diarrhoea," Gigi coughs out causing the whole class to laugh. They laugh as Susanna slams the door, tears rolling down her cheeks.

She runs to the girls' bathroom and locks herself in. After fifteen minutes a knock on the door forces her to open it. She finds Melanie looking at her from behind her black square frames. She is wearing a purple top over a pair of black jeans. Her black eyeliner is deeper than the other days. Her lips was painted plum, her trademark.

"You need to return to class," Melanie says looking above her glasses. "Prof. Cazz's orders."

"Coming," Susanna says but Melanie doesn't move. She shrugs then goes to the mirror and pretends to take something out of her eye. In the meantime Susanna washes her face.

"Have you ever thought about what you want for yourself instead of what that cretin wants?" Melanie says looking at Susanna through the mirror

"What?"

"Your weight." She turns and leans against the dirty sink to look at Susanna. "Do you think people are blind? That cretin was using you and you fell straight into his trap."

"What do you want from me?" Susanna sniffles. Melanie is annoying her.

"I wish all these stupid girls could stop wasting their time on that self-centred twat. Not that you are stupid."

Susanna wants Melanie out from the girls' bathroom "What do you know. Just be quiet, would you?" Susanna makes for the door, but before leaving she says "What do you know about love and Brad? I am sure if he asked you out, you would say yes!"

"No, he would be the last guy on earth I'd go out with. Just take care of yourself because you're much better than him."

Susanna leaves the bathroom without looking at her. Once in class she avoids looking at Brad. *If I lose a little bit more I'm sure Brad will like me then, obviously I haven't lost enough.*

CHAPTER 21

Life for Susanna accelerates to the speed of a bullet train, threatening a collision at the least distraction. To avoid eating at home, Susanna starts to go out with Natalie more often. Whilst Susanna's weight is on the decrease, her friend's is on the increase. Susanna notices how Natalie's weight is concentrated around her belly, but she can't bring herself to ask any questions. All she cares about is that, unlike her, Natalie doesn't have enough self-control to stop herself from getting fat. This makes her proud.

Susanna spends hours cutting all the pictures of skinny girls in the fashion magazines she now buys. She has a special notebook for the models with collarbones or hip bones sticking out, the more they're skinny the higher they're of her chart of beautiful. When she sees a curvy model in the magazine, Susanna cuts some part of the picture to re-shape the particular girl into a size she thinks looks nice. She reads new books and articles about dieting. In the end she comes up with a meal plan and schedule, which she obsessively adheres to. She allows herself no deviation. Not ever. If she goes to the store and doesn't find all the items on her shopping list, she shouts at the store keepers or she sit on the floor and sob. She spends more time at home than attending classes, Natalie's telephone calls are now being turned down again. She cares more about reading books and looking for new skinny models in the magazines than worrying about her friend, or any other problem for that matter.

Susanna's parents are worried, but they are powerless against Susanna's determination. Nelson makes a rough estimate of how much Susanna eats, and he concludes that she is consuming about two hundred calories a day.

Breakfast consist of a glass of water and a half piece of toast. School break she has a bite of small carrot. The purging worsens; she has to do it even if she drinks only water for the whole day. Each evening, after dinner, she waits until her parents are asleep to have a bath. These late baths allow her to purge. Her parents suspect it, but they can't fight back because her attitude and new-found voice make the situation intolerable for them to argue back. They are desperate but powerless in front of her new-found power of lightness.

CHAPTER 22
Asiago, Italy, December 1999

I walked past three girls smoking under the arch of the stadium. They looked as if they had been cut out from the pages of *Ragazza,* one of the teen fashion magazines I know Carla subscribed to. Their shiny straight hair, which didn't curl with a gust of wind, was tucked under red and gold wool hats. One girl in particular caught my attention. She was wearing a red mini skirt over bright stockings. At the sight of her slim toned legs, I felt a chill run down my spine. I tightly hugged my winter jacket.

I'd never been in a hockey stadium before. The first thing that hit my nose was the musty smell of old sweat. Then I noticed the dusty carpet and black grease on the light blue walls. Inside, instead of the soccer field's fluffy green, it was solid blueish-white ice. On the ice, the two teams, dressed in hockey socks, shin guards, and loose team jersey tops covering huge shoulder pads, were skating up and down, each player holding a long stick. After a few seconds looking around the stadium, I spotted Brad. He was wearing a red and gold jersey. His helmet was white with a red and gold eagle on each side. I nodded in his direction but he didn't see me because he was giving instructions to his team. I wanted him to see me before leaving the ice field so I found a seat above the lower passage that led into the changing room.

Minutes later I noticed the girls I'd seen outside going to

sit on the third row seat on the other side of the ice field. The one with the short skirt looked intently at Brad. I turned toward my boyfriend. For the first time I felt confident enough not to be jealous, because at the end of the game Brad Lawson, *my boyfriend*, was coming to me and not to anyone of those girls.

A couple of hours later, the cheers around me startled me back to the game, which I had not really been able to follow. Red and yellow flags were waving in the air. The girls on the other side were hugging each other, jumping up and down, holding their hats on their heads with one hand. I clapped my hands, a big grin across my face. Yet, I felt intimidated. I didn't have anyone to jump up and down with, even though my boyfriend's team had just crushed their opponent. I looked over the ice. Brad was holding his helmet up in the sky while pointing at the eagle. I felt proud to be his girlfriend. He blew a kiss toward the girls. My heart sunk. Few seconds later he skated towards the changing room. He saw me then, slowed down and waved at me. I bit a corner of my lower lip as I played with my right earring. My heart pumping more blood into my head when everyone turned in my direction. Some guys whistled as in cheering. I thought I saw all the girls in Asiago looking at me sideways. My cheeks were on fire.

"See you at the exit in fifteen." he said. I grin widened in reply. One of the guys skated into Brad. I thought Brad was going to fall, but he didn't; instead he turned and pulled the guy into a head lock. I watched them as they laughed, walking on their skates toward the changing room.

CHAPTER 23
Verona, Italy, April 2000

Easter Sunday, Susanna, together with Linda and their parents, go to their grandparents' villa for lunch. The sun is beaming, but Susanna wears a grandfather sweater and a loose pair of denims.

"Aren't you hot?" Linda asks when she sees her sister coming out of her room. Susanna shakes her head. For the rest of the journey she doesn't respond to anyone; instead, she becomes absorbed in the novel she's reading.

"The meal is served!" Prima, the cook, calls out when they arrive at their grandparents' house. Susanna runs her fingers though her hair, then bites her thumb. For starters, there is Parma ham and cantaloupe. The entree is pasta with shredded duck in cheese sauce. The main dish is *grigliata mista*, sausages, grilled steak and grilled chicken. As side dish there are boiled potatoes, salad and grated carrots. Susanna's stomach churns as the smell fills the dining room. She is hungry, but she pokes at everything without putting the fork in her mouth.

"What's wrong with your food?" her grandfather asks. Susanna stops playing with the food, looks up at him with a pleasant expression but doesn't say anything. She looks at Aunt Marta's plate. It's full of green leaves that she made Prima prepare especially for her. Susanna wishes she was old enough to do anything she wants with her food. *Aunt Marta is not eating anything but granddad won't tell her off, because she's an "adult".*

Her grandfather turns to her parents and asks "What's wrong with the *piccola*?"

"She's lost her appetite," her parents say in chorus. But the old man doesn't understand.

"Lost your appetite, Susanna? How can you lose your appetite?" Susanna frowns at her plate.

"*Papà*, it's not that easy," Susanna's mother chimes.

"What do you mean is not easy like that? Since when do people lose appetite? When the 1940s wars were upon us, we couldn't lose appetite. Food was not available to lose appetite over it. You better eat. Prima didn't cook to have it wasted and thrown in the bin." Susanna has never seen her grandfather so cross.

"*Papà*, leave her alone. She'll be fine" Marta defends Susanna. Susanna feels like breathing fresh air. "Susanna, here have some of this." Marta scoops two spoonful of boiled spinach.

"You don't understand, Marta! Susanna really needs medical help." her parents say finally but reluctantly.

Two weeks later.

I'm so annoyed with everyone! They won't let me be myself. My parents, again! I can't stand them.

They've forced me into this prison again. Just out of

the blue they decide *enough is enough*. It was just after a meal, when I went to my room to do my work out. I ran on the spot... the next thing I remember is waking up in this psychiatric unit of the Verona general hospital. My nightmare among all places!

When I came to my senses, I kicked and shouted, panic overtaking me. How can I get my workout done? How can I stick to my diet? These nurses will kill me. I've been crying non-stop. They can't understand the reason I don't like that girl in the mirror. They don't understand anything. A few days after I woke up from "death", as the *nice* doctor told my mother, they measured my heart rate. I was just over 40 bph, which was a good sign because I was picking up fairly quickly. Donna is the nurse assigned to me. Apparently my parents are embarrassed so they locked me in the private section again. I give Donna the evil eyes. I despise all of them for their work. I know they want me to be fat just like them. Forcing me to overeat, they say I have to get better, as if I'm ill.

Unlike the nurses from last month I was in the hospital, after I stupidly fainted on the bus, these nurses are so nice they make me sick. Though I curse Donna under my breath every day, she doesn't give.

One thing I like about being at the recovery centre is seeing other girls. I feel like I'm on a team. Most of us are here because some adult forced us into this shit hole. Trigger, the girl I met back in March, is still here. She is looking curvier, compared to last time and she seems happy *all the time*. There are also new girls; some are as young as eight, but we are all fighting together, we're not going to let the nurses make us fat.

I like going to group therapy, I hear all sort of life stories, but I haven't said a word since I arrived. Twice a week each patient has to talk privately with a psychiatrist for twenty minutes. I *hate* those days; I believe the psychiatrist needs help more than I do. Just looking at him makes me ill. Big spotty nose, his thin lips hidden by an untidy moustache, I can't imagine his wife kissing him. From the picture on his desk, she's sterile like him. She is probably a surgeon.

On our first visit after a few preliminary questions he asks, "Why are you here?"

I don't say a word, I look at him sideways.

He notes something in his notebook. He looks over his reading glasses and asks the next question.

"Do you want to be here?"

What a stupid question! Of course not, stupid man. I'm not ill in the first place and only mad people go see a shrink, not a sane girl. I look at him blankly. He asks the same question over and over again, but instead of answering, I just keep looking at him tiredly. I haven't being sleeping very well lately. I feel cold all the time and this place is making me really ill. As the psychiatrist looks at me for answers, I count the seconds on the watch on the white wall.

"Susanna, Susanna..." he calls my name a couple of times.

"Mmmm..."

"You have to talk, that's the only way to recover."

Recover from what? Who told you I want to recover at all. I like the way I am now, even if I need to lose a few inches. I don't care about Brad any longer. I'd rather be dead than go back to Susanna mandolin-bottom. I think that, but I don't say anything to the psychiatrist.

He says something else but my mind has switched off to another level. I only hear "...well, the twenty minutes are over..." Alleluia! "I guess..." He hesitates for a few seconds but then just says "See you next time." I get out of the room as quickly as I can.

"I don't understand those girls there..." Susanna overhears "Trigger" tell a curvy girl during breakfast one day. Susanna looks in the direction of some skinny girls sitting at the other end of the breakfast table. Trigger carries on the conversation. "I want to eat and get out of this shithole as soon as possible, but I don't think they want that. They cry at each mouthful as if they are desperate to be here." *I doubt anyone likes to be in this prison.* Susanna thinks while looking at her untouched meal.

"When I came here, I was, like, 35 kilos..." the curvy girl says.

Wow, I wish I was that weight. I haven't weighed myself in ages. I don't remember how much I weighed when I came here and, I'm sure I've doubled since. Susanna looks at her thighs.

"They don't understand how harmful it is losing weight the way we did. I'm twenty-three years old, but it took me seven years to accept the fact that I was ill and needed help."

"I came here as soon as I noticed my obsessive eating habits." Trigger takes a mouthful of her scrambled eggs and ham. She licks her lips then continues. "I liked it when people said I was 'superhot'. I really thought that to keep my appearance extreme dieting was the only option. Losing weight was not my goal; I was trying to be healthy but being slim became an obsession. I wouldn't eat anything apart from high fibre and chicken breast and salad. For instance, if at breakfast or dinner my mom cooked something different from what I requested, I would shout at her, or literally run to the gym as soon as possible even if I didn't eat the meal. Now, I can eat anything and enjoy the meal." She clicks her tongue on her teeth.

Susanna looks at her plate and wants to push it aside, but the kitchen nurse is observing her every move. So, forcing herself, she takes a mouthful.

Once out of the dining room, Susanna walks briskly to burn some calories, but a nurse notices and tells her to slow down. When she gets to her room, she finds a nurse going through her drawers. "What are you doing here?" Susanna is fuming.

"It's a routine search?"

"Why?"

"For your safety."

"My safety?" Susanna breathes deeply. "You're breaching my privacy."

The nurse turns to look at Susanna who is still standing in the doorway.

"Breaching your privacy, *principessa?* If you wanted privacy, you should have eaten the food you were served at home. It's routine procedure —. We know that most of you don't want to be here and it's likely that you have items that can be used to sabotage the therapeutic process."

"You, you, you… can't you stop putting all of us together? Anyways, I don't have anything. How can I hide anything when I'm under 24/7 surveillance?" Susanna rolls her eyes.

"*You* might not have anything to hide, but some of the other girls are experts in sabotage." The nurse is still going through the lower drawer. Susanna finds it hard to watch as her underwear and bras are picked up and then returned to the drawer. She sits up on the bed cross-legged, observing the nurse.

"What do they do?" Susanna asks referring to the girls whom sabotage their treatments.

"Nothing… mmm… Now, I'm done here." The nurse gets to her feet, flats down the crease out of her dress and walks to the door, but then turns to say, "Remember tomorrow morning, you have a blind weigh-in."

"Yes..." Susanna rolls her eyes at the ceiling. For safety, the girls are not allowed to have mirrors in their personal rooms, but Susanna can see herself in the reflections of the window panels. When she sees the image, she doesn't recognize the girl staring back at her. It scares her to feel such revulsion towards her own self. *I hate blind weigh-ins, I'm putting on weight and I can't tell how much. People think I am taking this recovery well, but I am collapsing more each day that passes. I hope somebody can see but nobody seems to care. What the nurses care about is me eating my meals without fuss. They just want me to get fat and get out of here. Maybe I should do just that. I can get skinny again once I'm out.* Susanna lets herself fall heavily onto the bed.

CHAPTER 24
Verona, Italy, June 2000

Two months since I've been locked in this shit hole, I've lost count of the exact days. Being here is the same story every time. Natalie comes to visit me once in a while. She still looks chubby around the belly, but I don't care. I have my own weight to lose to worry about hers. In my spare time, I go to the community library to escape my situation. I'm reading a book about a model who was recovering from anorexia.

Her story is making me question if my innocent diet restriction was after all that innocent. Her account of her fears of certain food, the calculations of food, the obsessions working out after each meal, the weight weighing and the mind control resonate so much with my old habits. I wonder if I'm... *sick*? ... *anorexia*? It's impossible. But then again her mood swings and dislike of her family is similar to my own emotions towards my family. I can't believe this is an illness. I am so strong, I've never being in my entire life. *How can I give up such strength?*

Yet, a part of me wants to recover to regain the happiness and love I felt when I was in the company of my family and Natalie. I want to enjoy my food, especially *tiramisu*. But no matter how hard I try, it's impossible.

I'm living in a state of daze, everything around me seems moving in slow motion. I fear closing my eyes at night, when I manage to close them for some hours – if I'm lucky, three hours – the images of Brad and me together overwhelm me. In these images he would tell me how he loves me and wishes we were still together. He apologises for all the hurtful things he allowed his friends to say to me. He circles my shoulders in a protective way and while caressing my hair says "You are so beautiful, Susanna. You are perfect, Susanna. Don't ever change… You're amazing, and I don't deserve you. Your body is beautiful, perfect and amazing the way it is, Susanna." Sometimes I wake up with tickling sensation in my stomach and between my legs, but soon enough the negative side of me tells me I don't deserve any of those beautiful words. I'm drowning.

CHAPTER 25
Asiago, Italy, December 1999

When we left the stadium, fresh snow had just started falling. I held tightly on Brad's waist for support. His scooter started after couple attempts. The wind felt like ice chips on my face. I hid my face in his jacket.

"Are you okay?" he patted my thigh.

"Gues… s… so…" I stuttered.

"Before we go to the *baita* I want to show you a magical place." Though the snow was not covering the street it was starting to fall heavily. *We're never going to be back in time*, I thought. He continued "My late Christmas gift for you."

"Mmmm… The snow?" I said, worried.

"Snow? Don't worry, we will get to the place and back to the chalet before the roads are totally covered," he said. The wind was penetrating my thick jacket. I was trembling from head to toe, especially with those flat shoes. After what felt like ages, he parked at the edge of the forest. Fear chill added to the cold chill. It looked as if we were the only souls out there.

"I can't see anything," I complained, my feet had started to turn into ice.

"We have to walk a little, you'll be fine." He reached one hand towards me.

"Really? I'm getting very cold with these flats." I clasped at the collar of my coat.

"Yep... knowing your taste... you'll like it. Trust me." He curled towards my face and kissed me not worrying one bit about how cold I was. "Are you scared?"

"A little." My breath was heavy in the air. Brad wrapped my shoulders with his arms and led me deep into the woods. The snow was soft under our shoes. A few steps later I saw a wooden hut in the darkness. I turned to look at Brad but he misunderstood my expression as excitement. He grinned. "I said you'll like it!"

"Mmmm!" It was all I could say.

"Do you like it then?"

"Nice." My mind was half frozen from the icy wind. He held my hand as he walked briskly toward the hut. I trotted behind him.

Inside was cosy, the wooden floor was covered in exotic rugs, in a corner there was a daybed on which laid a thick duvet covered with an East Indian print. In another end there was a smoking chair on which was piled tons of throws. On the walls were vintage pictures of Asiago and surrounding mountain towns. "I really it, whose place is it?" I ran my finger on the books on a little bookshelf.

"The guy who bumped into me at the ice rink when I was talking to you?" He came a bit closer to me and took my scarf off. "He owns this place. His parents live in the house next door."

"I didn't see any house apart from this hut."

"It's too dark to see. His name is Fabio." He paused and rubbed his fingers through his wet hair. "He said this place is really magical under the snow." He let out a laugh and wrapped my waist. He then whispered "Truth is... I begged him for this place."

"Why?" My heart skipped a beat or two.

"I wanted to be alone with you, enjoying the quiet before facing my loud friends." He kissed my ear then said "They are going to make a big deal about the game." He kissed my neck and run his lips down my collarbone. My heart had descended into my stomach, dancing with million butterflies. My whole body was trembling.

"Have you been here before?" I turned to him, I felt light headed.

"No... This is the first time. He's very protective of this place and never allows anyone to come over." His honey hazel eyes bared my soul. I swallowed the saliva that had formed in my mouth, wet my lips and stood on my toes to press my lips to his. Brad cupped my head in his hands and my chiffon came undone over my shoulders. I touched my hair, some part of the straightened hair had turned into curls. Still kissing me, Brad kicked a chair out of our way and led us to the daybed. I shivered when he took off my top, my camisole followed. I was left in my purple bra. He kissed the skin between my breasts.

"Oh... cute belly button –" Brad gently pressed his finger on my swollen belly button. That took me by surprise, I've always seen it as one of my biggest flaws. Then he said, "I like your belly, round and sexy like a belly dancer." He rubbed on the belly. I ran my fingers through his short hair. Brad helped me onto the daybed. I had a fixed smile on my face, I couldn't tell if I was dreaming or if it was really Brad whose hand was touching my legs, pinching my thighs. His lips running downward and investigating my body. I didn't know if the contrasting thoughts in my mind were normal. A part of me wanted to go all the way with him, but another part was afraid about what he was going to think about me. I looked into his eyes, he smiled and I knew I was ready to go to the next level in our relationship.

The snow was falling heavily on the window panels, I could hear the sandy noise. I circled my waist with Brad's arms. I took his head in my hand to look him in the eyes.

"Don't worry, I have a condom..." was all he cared about. I nodded but maybe he did read what was really playing in my mind because he said "... it won't hurt –"

Still my heart wasn't pacified. It played a noisy orchestra against Brad's heart which was playing rock 'n' roll. His *tum, tum, tum* against my *shuff, shuff, shuff* like a little foetus in his mother's womb at the first heart scan.

"I'm not scared..." I shook my head. I could feel my hot cheeks melting in his hands. "...I love you and I want you to be my first in everything..."

"Umm... Idem." He murmured between short breaths. That 'idem' could have meant many things, but my heart understood 'idem' as Brad loves me too. I circled his neck with my arms as he opened my jeans with his free hand, the other cupped on a breast.

CHAPTER 26

I wish I could say it was magical. Every time I think about that moment I feel sick. Once he was over me the dancing butterflies stood still. The pain was sharp but not everlasting. I tried to relax as much as possible to get over with the painful bit. It didn't feel like a scene from a romantic movie. Once he moved away from me, I sat on the daybed like a deflated balloon.

He dragged his jeans on and without looking at me said, "The snow will keep us here if we don't hurry." All I wanted was to throw up, instead I pulled my jeans on my legs and my top over my head. I pressed down my messy hair into my white woollen hat. Brad was already at the door.

On our way back to the youth chalet we didn't say much. In my mind, a little voice started to ask too many questions: *were you hoping Brad would be romantic? Cuddle you on that daybed? Was I any good? Am I too fat? Did my body turn him off? Were you hoping he would reassure himself that you liked it or felt something special? Were you ready? Did you feel pressured?* But there were no answers.

Soon Brad's scooter was parked in front of the chalet.

When I took my helmet off, I saw the blond girl with the mini skirt smoking by the front terrace. Brad looked up at her and they exchanged smiles. She turned away when I smiled at her. I focused my attention on the lyrics of the loud music coming from inside. I felt small as I followed Brad up the stairs, my stomach in knots. "*Hey* Brad... no *bacio?*" the miniskirt girl asked from the terrace as we entered.

"Stellaaaaa!" Brad shouted out her name as he went over to exchange warm mouth to cheek kisses. I noticed the way he held her waist a little bit too tight and rubbed his palm under the bomber jacket she was wearing. I hated her slim toned legs, her Barbie doll waist tightly squeezed into the red top and gold bomber. I hated her sleek blonde hair and her peachy glossy lips, which spouted like a diva as Brad greeted her. More than anything, I hated her name. *Her mother must have seen stars when giving birth to her.* "Did you see the way we killed those from Cortina?" Brad lifted her up. She giggled and held her skirt down.

"Where is the bathroom?" I wanted to get out of sight to calm my nerves because Brad looked too enthralled by Stella. My boyfriend turned to look at me as if he didn't see me there.

"Second door on the left." He pointed. As I turned I saw Stella whispering to Brad and they both laughed. At the scene, I nearly knocked over empty bottles which were lined up at the entrance.

I walked past a semi-closed door from which I heard some voices. I felt awkward and self-conscious. I was among people I barely knew and the guy I just...

I hurried into the bathroom and locked myself in. I went straight to the mirror. My hair was roughly tucked under the hat. I wet my face with warm water then applied some lip gloss to moist my lips. I couldn't help but compare myself to the blond girl outside with Brad.

My cheeks were fuller, my collarbone filled with flesh, not bony like hers. I didn't dare look at my doughy stomach and big butt. I took the hat off. My hair was a mess. Though I dampened my curls with water they wouldn't let themselves be tamed. They stuck out like Medusa hair. I put the hat back on. I didn't like the girl starring back at me. My round cheeks were warm again, I patted cold water and inhaled deeply. I sighed and went out.

"And you are?" a tall bald guy startled me as I got out of the bathroom. He was standing in front of a semi-closed door, which I assumed was the living room because many voices were coming from there, with a beer in hand.

"Susanna. I'm here with Brad," I said, looking over the guy's shoulder for Brad.

"Brad... hey Brad?" this guy kicked the door open and called my boyfriend out "Brad, is this the girl?"

"Yes, Volpe" Brad nodded and smirked.

"Bravo" Volpe said proudly. He looked older than the guys who had followed Brad into the hall.

"You know me, Volpe, patience and determination are a few of my qualities." Brad smirked again. Volpe looked please so I assumed he was happy for Brad for having a girlfriend like me. I smiled and made to greet him. He recoiled and pulled away.

"Ha. Ha. Ahahha!" Volpe laughed hysterically. The drops of sweat on his head shone under the corridor neo light. "You are polite compare to those animals I work with in the factory."

I turned to Brad. He stood against the wall with his hands tucked into his jeans pockets. He didn't smile, he just looked through me. I was feeling ill in the stomach, but I smiled to hide my feelings.

"What are you laughing about?" Volpe snapped at me. I felt the floor opening under my feet. *He is worse than Gigi*. I thought as I observed him in detail.

Volpe wasn't bald as I first thought. His hair was only cut extremely short, close to the scull. He wore a t-shirt rolled up to show off his tattoos. They stretched from the neck down to the arms. They were skulls wearing military helmets that look very similar to those worn by the Nazi soldiers during the Second World War. I wanted to get out of that place, but Volpe hadn't finished with me.

"What does your father do again?" He was not really asking me a question because he said, "... the banker, eh?! A *nigger*, as a banker!" He laughed more and the other guys joined in. Stella was standing next to Brad. "Which one of us has a monkey banker for a daddy?" Volpe turned his question to the crowd.

"*Nessuno!*" the guys answered in a chorus.

"Right! *Nobody*... but wait this *pretty* girl's daddy is a monkey banker!" Volpe came too close, a sharp smell of alcohol punched my face. "Yes, you hear right... your *nigger* daddy is the only one who works in a bank. You are the only one whose father is a *nigger* banker. Look around, you don't belong here. Your father doesn't belong here... not in this country. How did he get here anyhow?" It was clear he had his mind made up about my father and didn't want my answer. "He was on one of those boats from Africa to Italy. The one you hear news about every day on channel 5, right?"

My heart sank down into my stomach. It stayed there for few seconds. I really thought I'd drown in that corridor until I heard my voice say "No, he came here on a plane from London"

"Shut up, fat bitch! Who asked you to open your *nigger* mouth?" His saliva spat onto my cheek. I wiped my face with my sleeve, while fighting back tears. I felt my body shrinking against the wall. Brad was silent the whole time. He wouldn't look at me, even though I was desperately searching for his eyes. After a while I looked at the dirt on the wooden floor.

Volpe kept on going "This country was founded on the shoulders of hard labourers and not easy money makers like your nigger daddy and the whole lot of your family." I looked up at him, he was red in the face as he carried on "I work in the factory... wake up at five o'clock. A quick cup of coffee for breakfast. Then I stand in front of a hundred centigrade heat for eight hours. In the meantime your father turns and twists next to his white rich bitch of a wife. That *puttana*... she didn't like one of her own. She wanted something *exotic*." Volpe was towering over me. It was only at this point that Brad moved forward to prevent him from crashing me. I pushed my way through the 'spectators' and fled that hell. My hand couldn't grab the door handle fast enough because Stella pulled my hair and said, "Her hair is soft, it's not as coarse as her *negra* friend." Drops of tears dribbled down my cheeks, my heart felt like a lost ship at sea.

"It must be a wig from Viale Mazzini bought with the money of *nonno*? Sleeping with a nigger disgusts me. At least Brad just had a little bit of fun with you, eh?" Volpe's words arrowed at my back. From the corner of my eyes I saw Brad looking at me, but I didn't have the courage to return his gaze. *How could I have been so stupid to believe every word he said?* I felt like dying as I descended the stairs. As I ran, a repressed image of children chanting in a foreign language crystallized in my mind.

CHAPTER 27
Kumasi, Ghana, December 1989

I'm six years old. I'm in Ghana for Christmas holidays with Daddy's family. I love Granny Margaret, I like the way she doesn't pull my hair when she braids it. Unlike my mom or the hairdresser, Granny Margaret takes her time washing my head and makes sure drops of water don't get into my eyes or ears. She then holds the root of my hair when combing so it doesn't pull. I like the way she turns my hair in her soft, buttery hands.

The night before Christmas, it's tradition for the children of the area go around to the houses in the neighbourhood asking for sweets. That night, after my granny had done my hair, I insist on joining in the fun. I take a yellow wicker basket with me. It is one of the gifts my grandfather bought me for Christmas from the Wood Toy shop in Asiago.

As soon as Abena, the older kid that tells everyone around what to do, sees me, she shouts in her broken English "Because you are from *abroad* doesn't make you special in anyway."

"I'm not special. I just want to be friends," I say in my nicest voice

"Can I touch your hair?" another child, Becca, ventured. I normally don't like when people touch my hair because in Verona all my class mates did that to hurt me. But her smile encourages me to lean my head towards her.

"Look at her hair. She is always touching it because she

thinks she is prettier than us. She might be white and her hair falls straight back down but she's not a pretty. You are not a pretty, go away from us. You don't belong here. There's no one who looks like you," Becca says, then she pulls my hair. I scream in pain.

Abena points out "She's not a proper white. Her mother is the real white –" she laughs revealing her decayed tooth.

"You are right. *Obroni pete!*" Becca says in Ghanaian. She stands there one hand on the waist.

"*Obroni pete ko, obroni pete ko...*" Abena starts to sing, some of the children join in the chorus "*Obroni pete ko, obroni ko ocrom.*" Some of the children join in the chorus "*Obroni pete fi a ko, ye duane an so ye di na wa beyi a di.*" Obroni Pete, Obroni Pete; I don't understand the words but Abena's frowning eyes tell me what she wants me to know. She looks at me up and down and then *cccchewwws* me through her teeth.

As I run to my grandmother's house, the unknown words arrow after me. "*Obroni pete!* OBRONI PETE!" Tears stream down my cheeks while the warm African Christmas air dry the drops making my face sticky.

CHAPTER 28

Those words chanted at me ten years before suddenly are a blazing meteorite bringing me down. At sixteen, I've come to understand enough Ghanaian to translate Abena's song. *Fake white go away, fake white you don't belong here, fake white go to your home, our food is not enough for you to come and eat it.* Those words sounded like Volpe's words *Nigger you don't belong here... we work hard here, and you swim in the gold because that bitch of a white married a nigger.* Obroni Pete-Negra Obroni Pete-Negra Fake White-Nigger Obroni Pete-Negra....*Where do I belong? Where do I stand on the social scale?* I couldn't answer and it was not going to be easy for me to find an answer. I didn't want to forget both experiences. As I walked down the stairs of the *baita* the scene that followed the run to my grabby house ten years earlier came back to me.

I run straight into my granny's arms. Once in her lap, granny Margaret's soothing voice hushs me in Ghanaian.

"*Odo, mensu...*" I love her sing-song voice but I look at her confused as I fight for breath. "Love, don't cry... you are here with your granny who loves you dearly," she says in English. I lay my head on her chest. I sniff. My granny wipes my nose with her fingers. "*Odo*, what happened?" I imitate to her how Abena looked at me, but I can't remember the exact words Abena used. I can't explain to my granny the burning I felt inside.

165

That night granny tucks me into bed, but I can't sleep. I stay awake the whole night, fighting against my tired eyes. I want to ask Father Christmas why those children see me differently.

Father Christmas never shows up.

Ten years later, I know better to wait for an answer from Father Christmas.

The snow was falling thick on the street. The cars and the scooters in the parking lot are covered. In the place where Brad's scooter was, is a valley of snow. I pulled the hood of my jacket over my head. I looked up in the sky but all I could see was a thick white blanket of shaken white flakes. I stuck my tongue out to catch one. I turned to look at the veranda hoping to see Brad coming after me, but he wasn't there. I wanted to wake up from that nightmare. I pinched myself but I was awake.

I put on the gloves I had in my pocket. I thought about granny Margaret reassuring me with her soothing voice. As I reached the last stairs I decided to find the answer for myself. I turned to look at the door once again. The snow fell on my face, I opened my arms to embrace its fragility. I knew the way home was long, but I didn't care because I needed to walk to clear my mind. The cold European Christmas air froze the drops making my face sting.

CHAPTER 29
Verona, Italy, June 2000

One day Linda surprises her little sister during visiting hours. Susanna is not waiting for a visitor, when she sees Linda walking into the common room, she's not happy. Linda is wearing a long red vintage top, over white skinny jeans and sandy sandals. Her curls are pulled up into a ponytail enhancing her beautiful oval face. Today Susanna is wearing her electric blue Addidas tracksuit, her hair is pulled into a scruffy ponytail. She feels like a tramp in comparison to Linda. Susanna pulls away when Linda makes to hug.

Linda is silent. She looks at her wicker bag to avoid staring at her once bubbly little sister. Deep down, Susanna is happy to see Linda but another part of her doesn't want her there because she feels judged.

"How are you doing?" Linda smiles from across the table.

"How would you feel if you were sent to prison against your will?... Ecstatic! Euphoric!... *ED-listic!*"

"What means *ED-listic?*" Linda smiles hoping her sister will warm up.

"If you want to know, it's just the acronym of Eating Disorder." Susanna snaps.

"What's your problem? There's no need for that cross tone with me." Linda's words scratch something in Susanna because suddenly she feels the urge to hurt her sister's feelings even more.

"It's *your* fault I'm here."

"You blame me? I wasn't home when you collapsed the third time, Susanna."

"If you didn't tell Mom and Dad about the second time I collapsed, I wouldn't be here." She leans forward, fisting her hands.

"I hate the way you are right now. You were so fun before this thing..."

"Thank you very much. I hate you too Linda..."

"Look... I didn't come here to fight." Linda bites her lower lip "If you don't want to talk... I'll come another time."

"Whatever." Susanna waves her hand in the air as she looks down at the table.

Linda's eyes are red with tears. Before leaving she puts a leather diary on the table. Susanna looks away. Linda looks at her sister quietly then says: "I love you very much... and I miss my funny sister. The one who used to tease me about my boyfriends and music... I hate to see you consumed by this thing... Hating me is nothing compared to how much I pray you get back to your old self. And if blaming me will make you feel better... do so. I'm ready to do anything to see you smiling again." Linda wipes her cheek. Susanna frowns, looks at the diary on the other side of the table. She bites her nails. It hurts her to see the sandy sandals turn and leave the common room, but she can't take back the words.

CHAPTER 30

Susanna runs to her bedroom, leaving the diary on the table. Nobody stops her, they all witnessed the heated exchange with Linda. For the first time since her recovery, Susanna doesn't care if people see tears roll down her cheeks. In a way, it's liberating.

Once in her room she falls heavily on the bed. Lately to feel alive, she lets herself drop onto her bed for as long as she can. Today she does that; then she punches the pillows several times. That's the only thing the nurses can't prevent her from doing. She doesn't wipe the tears which have formed a river under her cheeks and stained the pillows. She's misses her family. She misses her old self: the Susanna who laughed with her family without feeling the need to shout at them for no reason.

Linda's words ring in her ears as she hides her face in the wet pillow. *I hate to see you consumed by this* thing… *hating me is nothing compared to how much I pray you get back to your old self.* She knows what the *thing* is… ED or eating disorder, is the thing. She can't believe how this *thing* can hide so well the love she feels for her sister. *I hate ED for what is doing to my emotions. I hate ED for making me shout at my beloved sister. I miss her so much, yet when she comes to visit after nearly three months without talking, I treat her like shit… How much I hate myself.*

She cries so hard. She feels as if her head is about to explode but she doesn't care, because her mind registers each dropped tear as a way to help her lose weight. Somebody knocks on the door.

"Look at you." Trigger says. Susanna looks up. Trigger looks beautiful with her bright lipstick and her eyelashes curled to perfection with a thick mascara. "Look at you in your little princess dungeon. I wish I had a room all for myself instead of sharing with that new girl. Did you know she wets her bed? She gets up early and washes her mess, that's why we see her so early every morning." Susanna lets out a faint laugh. Trigger continues with her comic tone, "But once you make the stink, it remains in the air. Every morning I spray the room with my perfume but it doesn't help because it is call *odore d'toilette*, smell of toilet. Her wee and my perfume make a bad chemical reaction."

Susanna bursts out laughing, it hurt her stomach, but the facility with which she laughs surprises her. *Gosh, I haven't laughed like this in ages.* Although she's hasn't talked with 'Trigger' much, she feels so connected to her. She likes her company.

"I'm Susanna."

"And I'm Veronica"

"Thanks for letting me know who to stay away from," Susanna says sitting on the bed

"Oh, I don't want you to stay away from her. In fact you should talk to her, if you have any suggestions to get her to stop her bad habit, which is killing me. Please, I would like to know." Veronica smiles and hands Linda's gift to Susanna.

"Oh, thanks." Susanna takes the diary and absently turns the pages. A floral envelop falls out, she picks it and holds it up. After a little pause she says, "That was my sister."

"Beautiful girl," Veronica winks. Susanna keeps her eyes fixed on the floral envelop. "Why are you cross with her?"

"'I'm not…" Susanna wants to lie but then out of the blue says, "It's her fault I'm here."

"Are you cross because she wants to save your life?" Veronica's tone is gentle "I wish my family cared enough about me to send me here." Susanna looks up at her "This is the third time I've been here and each time I fall, I have to bring myself up alone. Nobody tells me to get a grip on my life. I don't know why I'm even telling you this. I'm such a bad example. I'm scared of the outside world because, for most of the battle against this illness I've been alone." She stops for a few seconds before saying, "Well, nice space you have here. Take care."

"Really nice talking to you." Susanna looks up and curls her lips in a smile.

"No worries." Veronica winks at Susanna and closes the door behind her. Susanna stares at the door for more than five minutes after she's gone. *I wish she was still talking to me. I like her voice.* For the first time in months, Susanna craves human company.

That night, when Susanna finds herself drowning with her own thoughts, she opens the floral envelop she found in the diary. She recognises Natalie's neat feminine handwriting.

Ciao Susah, I hope my letter finds you well. I'm finally fine again. I don't know how to write a letter to you. I would rather draw but I know it's not right to simply doddle a big news.

Also I've never written you a proper letter before because we were always on the phone or in each other's company before this year. So much has changed for both of us.

This is like the hundred time I'm trying to spill out everything but I'm finding it hard to get the right words.

Maybe you noticed but were polite not to say anything. The last time I came to visit you I was looking so heavy around the belly because I was pregnant. Even though then I knew something wasn't right with me I didn't want to believe it until I went into labour couple days after my visit.

When I told William about the situation he was so nice and wanted to be part of the whole journey. He was there when I gave birth (he says to tell you hi :). On the other hand my mother doesn't want to see me again. She says I'm a disgrace. I can't blame her, she's such a believer of good principles, marriage before children. My father is okay with the situation, bless his heart.

I can't believe that I'm a mother at seventeen. My baby boy is called Nathan, it's a Hebrew name that means Gift from God. We chose the name because William's family is from Israel and I believe life is a wonderful gift that comes from Almighty. We're so happy to have a precious gift as my baby boy Nathan. He's so cute with a dimple in his chin, I love him is impossible to describe.

We're living with William's family. They're such a happy family, I'm learning new ways of living but some of their traditions remind me of the Ghanaian traditions, such as circumcision (I know you don't care about these things but these are few of the things I have to start thinking about).

I'm getting too long. I can't wait to show you Nathan. By the way, want it or not, you're the godmother of my precious boy. Your godson sends you lots of love and sweet kiss.

Hear you soon,

Your one and only Nat.

After Susanna finishes reading her best friend's letter, she writes a phrase in capital letters in her new diary: I want to love myself, to be present for my family and my best friend again! I want the old Susanna back into my life!

CHAPTER 31
Verona, Italy, December 1999

27-12-'99

I need to write it down. I don't know where to turn but unto these pages. I just got home from my evening with Brad. I don't know if it was a dream or a nightmare. I feel like closing my eyes, maybe the pain will go away and I will wake up to find out everything was a bad, bad dream.

28-12-'99

I just woke up with hot flashes of last night, events on my mind. Brad and me, in the cosy hut. Brad's friends in the chalet. Their words sting... I'm not sure if 'm just having a nightmare or what happened last night is real. I'm slapping my face and pulling my hair. Tears are smudging the pages as I write. But I can't stop crying.

I was lucky my grandparents' friend, Sig. Gina, saw me when I got out of the youth chalet. I don't know if I would be alive now. I thanked my lucky star when I saw her car approaching. By the time I reached the main road, I was so cold I couldn't walk any further. When she asked me what I was doing walking in the snow, I didn't say a thing, my words were frozen. I just complained on and on about how snow had ruined my make-up and hair.

Who am I? Do I feel more black or white? I don't know! I DON'T know! I never thought about my colour so much as I am thinking about it now. COLOUR? Who invented the colour classification anyway? I never thought of dad as being black or mom as white. What is a skin colour in the end? It's just melanin, isn't it?

Why can't I just be Susanna Danso? I don't see my father black or my mother white, all I care about is that I am their daughter and that they love me. But now I know that when I am with my mother some people think I am white and when I am with my father I am black, or *nigger* as Volpe called me yesterday. When will people stop looking at me as a colour instead of as a person? Do I have to be ashamed because I don't want to be in a box? Do I have to be ashamed because I want to be just a human being? When did colour classifications become so popular? Why can't I just be Susanna Danso?

2:30p! My thoughts are twirling over themselves over and over.

I can't stand this life anymore. I wish I could do something as creative as Linda. She can play the piano and write amazing songs. I don't have any ability... I'm just a waste of space... I hate myself, I can't look at myself in the mirror. Obviously, Brad couldn't look at me last night, I hate myself so much. My head is pounding and I don't know what to do to make it quiet.

I can't get Brad's face out of my mind. I can feel his hands through my hair. He is MY FIRST, MY FIRST in everything. Maybe I should look like Stella, they would like me more. How could his friends be so cruel? I miss Brad so much. I phoned him this morning but his sister said he's still out. I'm sure he came home last night.

My eyes are burning. What's the point writing when all the tears are smudging the words? I can't write properly. I feel like dying. I want to go out in the snow and bury myself alive. I WANT TO DIE. I really want to DIE! I'm ashamed, he saw everything of me and he didn't like... I would be happier dead than alive. My stomach is in knots. I'm lost.

I love you BRAD LAWSON! Brad, you are my only love... I will try call him again.

Not home. I don't know what to do. Linda doesn't want to drive me to his apartment... I feel like he is home but he doesn't want to answer the call. I'm sure he is sorry for what happened yesterday and feels too embarrassed to talk to me.

But I have forgotten all the episodes. It is not his fault

if his friends are stupid. I don't blame him. I didn't have an appetite at lunch. My parents wanted to know the reason. They asked me why I walked home last night. I told them Brad and his friends were going to another place and I didn't want to go with them, but I was lucky to get a ride from Sig.ra Gina...

I can't see the pages, tears are blurring my vision. I wish Brad was here next to me, but he will not even receive my calls. Oh Brad, Brad Lawson do you how much I love you? I love you SO, SO much. Please, don't listen to Volpe and forget about our wonderful time together. I really love you, I love YOU!...............

29-12-'99
Yesterday I didn't sleep well. I couldn't stop writing the words I LOVE YOU. I wanted Brad to feel my love from all that distance, but my mind couldn't clear off the images of ~~Bella~~ Stella and Brad. I am sure he's used to skinny girls like her; both her legs can fit one leg of

my jeans. I remember the guys looking at her at the hockey game every time she stood up to cheer them. Her legs don't touch each other like mine. I saw the bones of her shoulders through her sweater when she took the jacket off. OMG, now I remember. I saw Brad looking at her when Volpe was saying all those words, making me feel as if I was a wild animal in a zoo. I feel ugly! I feel as if I've been stripped off my identity. I am so confused. Every time I try to write about the pain I am going through, tears block my vision and my thoughts blur together, I feel LOST!

30-12-'99

This morning I went for a walk in the woods. While I was walking I thought about Volpe's words. His monologue blurs into the echoes of laughter which followed each comment he made. The words keep coming back to me, cutting through my heart and soul. When I got back from the walk, I tried to phone Brad but his sister told me he was at a bar near the ice rink with some of his friends. I took the courage to go see him in person. I wore a white loose jeans and a deep red bomber jacket. I wanted to impress Brad so I left my hair loose on the shoulders, he always complimented me with my hair down.

When I arrived, I saw him standing in front of the bar talking to a group of guys. One of the guys pointed his head at me. Brad turned, his teeth set. He looked more handsome than I remember, maybe the tears have cleared my vision and I see more beauty in others but less in myself. My breath stood still for a second. I breathed in encouraging air and said,

"Can I speak to you for a second?"

"What do you want?" his voice was sharp.

"Can we speak? In private?" I kept my nerves under control, but I was close to tears.

"I don't want to talk to you." He snapped turning to look at the guys who were laughing under their breath. My face was burning. He followed up with "Look, I don't want to see you anymore, you are not my type. I'm into the sporty kind!" he winked at the group then said, "You look pregnant." The group laughed. My surroundings started to spin. I don't get it, how can he say such words to me? How? I didn't see this coming from Brad, breaking my heart in half like that. I didn't mind letting Volpe's harsh words wash over me, but hearing those words from Brad was like hot blade cutting on my bare back. When I turned to leave Brad shouted "Another thing –" I didn't want him to see the tears on my cheeks. But his words like bullets hit my ego on its knees "Come back when you look like a model." laughter followed.

Brad, the one I gave all myself to. Brad, the one who is my first in everything... No, I don't want him to be the first one to break my heart. *No, I am not fat, I am not fat... some of my clothes are the small size. I prefer to be comfortable so I buy medium sizes. My weight is right for my height. The doctor told me at my last appointment.* I know I am not slim like a stick, but I am not fat like a whale, either. But I can't black out Brad's words. I feel the world falling on me. I feel so low.

What a Christmas to forget!

I hid in my bedroom, I couldn't tell anyone what happened to me two nights ago. I felt ashamed. I wanted to hurt myself, I let myself fall heavily on the bed. I slid down off the bed hitting my head on the floor. I repeated the action for the past hour but it didn't take the pain away. I went to the bathroom to get rid of the nausea that suddenly came over me. I threw up, taking extra care not to let anything come out of the toilet. My head spun by the time I decided to stop. Linda came in my room and she convinced me to tell her half of the story. I told her about the game and how Volpe teased me. I avoided mentioning what Brad and I did.

31-12-'99

New Year Resolution.

Today I stopped crying. I have a plan and I need to focus. There are two days left before 2000. As they say: a new year, a new me. I want to be positive in the New Year. Normally, I don't write New Year resolutions but this time I want to write my wishes. I have three wishes. I hope they come true.

I want to lose weight and be skinny like a model. Now I am 58 kg.

I want Brad to like me again. To *desire* me so much he can't think about other girls.

I want to become a model, so those who hate me will eat their words and envy me. I want to show them that I too can the beautiful, sporty and slim like the models on a teen magazine.

My mother's latest issue of *Silhouette* magazine is lying around. It is perfect for what I need to achieve by next year – January 6th. There is an article for those who want to lose the extra weight accumulated over Christmas holidays.

I know my mother is going to do the same diet, she will not question my new eating habit, because she will be worried about her own food intake. All I have to be careful about are the vigilant eyes of my father and Linda.

My dieting journey begins tomorrow!

I was excited for the New Year. I wrote my wishes for the first time and with all my fingers and toes crossed I hoped my wishes came true: get back together with Brad.

I planned to lose two kilos for the first week. I wanted to look a little bit different when school started on the 6th.

Day one was a success, I cut down my portions. For breakfast I had water and a piece of apple. In the morning nobody was home so it was easy to stay away from the fridge. Lunch was challenging because I was sitting between Aunt Marta and Linda. I was convinced that Marta would have pointed out that I wasn't eating, so I ate everything on my plate. Normally I would have a snack around four, but this time I didn't. Instead I read a magazine, taking note of which of the models is skinnier than the other. One article promised to help anyone achieve a slimmer body in 7 days. The model looked like Stella, Brad's friend. Her body was the perfect slim hour glass. Small waist, flat tummy, slim thighs and arms. She looked like a surfer, dirty blond hair and honey gold skin tone. I wanted to be just like her. I cut out her image and put it into my notebook to remind myself of the goal.

In the evening my grandmother said "Susanna, you are not eating your dessert. I thought *tiramisu* is one of your favourites."

"Oh yes, I like it, but I had a big snack in the afternoon,

I'm so full." I rubbed my belly which was making so much noise under the table. If they listened hard enough they would have heard it too. But each rumble positioned me closer to winning back Brad.

As I wrote my diary later on that evening, my stomach was churning, telling me to go in the kitchen, instead I joined my family in the living room to do the countdown for the beginning of the New Year.

CHAPTER 32
Verona, Italy, July 2000

One day Susanna wakes up in a pool of blood. She screams so loudly that Donna, who was in the next room, comes running. One of the hospital's rules to be able to stay in therapy is *no self-harming*. She pulls the clean part of her bed sheet to her chest. She knows that her body is changing, getting heavier but if she wants to be out of that hospital the only thing for her to do is to eat well. She came to this conclusion after she read the book about a girl recovering from anorexia, and listened to what Trigger, who Susanna has started calling by her real name Veronica, had to say.

"I didn't do anything to myself," she says even before Donna can come up to the bed. "I'm sorry, I don't know what happened."

"What's the matter, Susanna?" Donna covers her mouth to hide a smile when she is close enough to see the problem. She's about to comfort Susanna, but Trigger comes into the room.

"Silly girl, that's your period."

Heat spread over Susanna's face. *How silly of me, I almost forgot about my period.*

"You can have a baby if you have sex with a guy." Trigger giggles.

Donna pushes her out of the room. "Don't listen to her."

But Trigger's words drill in Susanna's ears. *I don't want to have a baby.* She thinks about Natalie and her new baby she described in her letter. She feels the walls closing in on her. She remembers how the model in the autobiography she's been reading describes missing her period during the time her anorexia was at its peak. In that moment, Susanna wants to give up recovery for the sake of not having her period around.

"Everything will be fine. I know it's your first time, don't worry the blood will go away within a week, so don't worry. Now go take a shower. Then look under the sink, you'll find some pads. Take one and put on your underwear. It will soak the blood. Repeat that every couple of hours and you'll be fine." Donna, who has become very close to Susanna, rubs her fingers on Susanna's curls.

Before breakfast Susanna gets weighed. The nurse who usually does the weighing is on holiday. When she enters the clinic, the new nurse smiles at her but Susanna doesn't return the friendly smile. She gets all naked save for her underwear and bra.

"Stand facing the wall." The nurse says. After fidgeting with the scale. "Good. It's looking good. You are out of risk, — you are sixty kilos. From your records, you came here when you were below forty-seven kilos, which is around 104lbs. If you maintain this weight for at least two weeks, you can get out of the hospital." Susanna feels a sack of stones in the stomach when the nurse carries on, "You are getting healthier by the second."

Am I supposed to know this? Her eyes trace down her bulging belly and growing breasts. *I don't want to get healthy if getting healthy means having my thighs rub each other. I want to be ill for life, if being ill means not having thighs that rub each other, and NO PERIOD.* Susanna runs to her room and straight under cold shower. She read somewhere that cold water shrinks the fatty tissues.

At breakfast she looks at her food without touching anything. She doesn't feel like eating. The spoon looks like a gun ready to shoot her. Veronica, who is sitting next to her, notices and asks, "Everything okay?" and with her head points at Susanna's plate.

Susanna ignores her but Veronica, who doesn't let anything stop her, says "Are you sad because I'm getting out tomorrow?"

Susanna shoots her head up, eyes wide open. She didn't know about Veronica's sudden departure. Fresh tears start to stream down her cheeks, but still she doesn't say anything. There is always a nurse sitting at the entrance, supervising the girls while they eat. As if they wanted to make a statement, most of these nurses are on the heavy side of the scale. When she sees Susanna crying, she comes to stand behind her.

"What's wrong with your food?"

Susanna looks up at the nurse and sees a whale over her. "I don't want to be fat," Susanna yells, pushing her untouched plate onto the floor. Eggs and ham splatter everywhere. "I don't want to be a whale... All this shithole cares about is maintaining the 'ideal' weight. What if my 'ideal' weight is different from what the chart proclaims. I hate it when my thighs rub together."

The nurse's face is red, but she keeps a professional voice as she says "You have to eat what is on your plate, without question, that's the rule."

"Are you okay?" Trigger comes to hug Susanna. Susanna shakes her head, a sharp pain piercing through her chest. Trigger rubs her friend's shoulders as she says to the nurse, "Can you let her off this time? She eats everything on the plate, every time..."

"Rules are rules..." The nurse bites the dry skin off her lips then says, "She has to talk to the head." She turns impatiently on her rubber crocs and marches back to her seat.

"What is the matter, Susanna?" Doctor Gaetano, the head doctor of the psychiatric department of V erona Hospital, asks her once Susanna is seated in her office chair. Susanna doesn't answer. She stares at her. She is one of the few people working in the hospital Susanna secretly admires. Though she wears the same boring white coats all doctors wear, her spectacles tell a different story about her character. Today she is wearing red plastic frames, with floral details on the left side of the rim. Her strawberry blond hair is pulled into a tidy chiffon but wavy tufts have found their way out.

Today, her usual friendly smile annoys Susanna. She looks down at her own un-manicured nails to avoid Dr. Gaetano's deep green eyes.

The urge to bite her nails till they bleed is strong; instead she folds her hands in her lap. After a long silence, Dr. Gaetano says, "Susanna, we're here to help, but you have to talk. I heard you don't like talking to your private therapist."

Susanna shrugs, sucks her lower lip into her mouth, then bites her thumb nail.

Dr. Gaetano continues her monologue. "And today you decided not to have breakfast. Is everything okay?"

"I don't need help. I'm already above my ideal weight. I'm fine." Susanna crosses her arms on her chest and frowns at Dr. Gaetano.

"Who told you're fine?" Dr. Gaetano asks stretching her arms on the desk

"The nurse, this morning. She told me I've put on enough weight to leave the hospital."

"I'm sure she didn't mean what she said."

"But – "

"Susanna, you should know few things." Dr. Gaetano stops her. "First, having your weight at the right number doesn't necessarily mean you're healthy. Apart from achieving the right weight for your height and age, there is more to do before getting well and before we can discharge a patient." The doctor leans her chin on her clasped fingers.

"What if my ideal weight is different from what you believe is the right weight for me?"

Dr. Gaetano lets out a laugh then says, "We will never go

over your ideal weight. But to help you recover from your eating disorder we need to get to the root of the problem, and you're not making that possible."

Susanna looks down at her trainers to avoid eye contact.

"We can change the food choices but you have to eat the recommended calories. You are not going to become over weight. That's not our aim when we have a patient in therapy. We want you to be healthy both in mind and body."

"But being healthy means becoming fat." Susanna challenges Dr. Gaetano.

"You're not fat. You're eating well and getting your energy level high. As I said, our priority is for you to get well physically and mentally."

"You're just saying I should get fat and calm before you can discharge me." Susanna wasn't trying to be funny but Dr. Gaetano laughs lightly. She then brings her folded arms onto her chest and relaxes in her office chair.

"Oh no, no, that is not our aim. Treating an eating disorder is not about getting you to a weight and letting you go. Our aim is to ensure the health of your mind. We have to help you reach a balance between how you really see yourself and how you imagine yourself."

God, I hate philosophical talk. Susanna thinks as Dr. Gaetano says, "I will talk to you another time. You need to get back to the group therapy. You don't want to miss it, do you?"

After this short conversation Susanna feels a sense of complicity between them.

"No, today is the last day for Trigger."

"Trigger?"

"I mean Veronica."

"Aha. Before you go, take this." Dr. Gaetano takes an apple from a fruit bowl on her desk, she hands it to Susanna. "Have a bite. You need your vitamins after all." Susanna takes a bite from the apple in front of her. She smiles and hunches her shoulders. Dr. Gaetano smiles back.

Susanna steps out of the office feeling a bit cheerful. She thinks about how life can change in such a short space of time. The image of Brad is so feeble it seems as if he never existed but he was the genesis of her dark journey through eating disorder. Images of them together play on her mind but this time they don't make her sad.

CHAPTER 33
Verona, Italy, January 2000

01-01-2000

The sky was grey this morning. I weighed 57.5kg. Felt happy! I was so glad I didn't eat snack and dessert the day before. It was hard in the evening while everyone was counting and laughing, my stomach was grumbling. I read somewhere in a magazine that the first few days of a new diet regime are the hardest. Day two was going to be easier. For breakfast I had water with lemon, a handful of cereal and skimmed milk. At lunch I reduced my portion and ate everything. I avoided snack. For dinner we ordered pizza. I had small margarita. I didn't eat the sponge cake *pan Prima* prepared. Nobody noticed, but my stomach did. I could already feel less soft skin around the waist.

03-01-2000

Yesterday I was tired so I didn't update the diary. I weigh 57kg. I haven't made much progress over the past two days. I need to do something else. I thought it was going to be difficult to cut out dessert, but I am proud to say I am doing well. Not eating dessert is so empowering. If I can stop eating dessert, one of my favourite things ever, then I can eliminate any other food I don't like, for instance fast food and snacks. Soon I'll look like a model and Brad will come running to me.

This morning before my shower I looked at myself carefully in the mirror. I look so fat. For mental power I envisage my body to be lean like Stella's. I want her bony hips, skinny thighs, bony shoulders... I hate myself. She is so beautiful and skinny like Kate Moss. These thoughts sing a serenade to my grumbling stomach each night.

04-01-2000

Last night I was about to give up. I felt the urge to go downstairs for the piece of *tiramisu* I didn't eat for dessert, but counting imaginary stars soothed me to sleep.

So imagine my frustration when I woke up to be the same weight as yesterday.

I wonder how models can be so skinny. I want to learn their secret. They look so perfect, all the time even when they say they eat everything. Some say they have it in the genes, but I am sure it's not true. I want to learn how to be perfect like a model. Yes, I am obsessed with models. It feels good to have somebody to look up to.

Auntie Marta left for Verona today. As soon as the wheels of her car slid off, I ran into her room. She has a good selection of books on style, model autobiographies, fashion, photo shoots, food and decoration. On one of her bedside tables there are coffee table books with models posing in strange, x-rated positions. Other models are so skinny I can see their spine bone coming out from their stretched skin. They remind me of Jew victims during the Second World War. It's so strange how every time I involuntarily see pictures like those, the smell of burnt skin forces up my nose. I slammed the book close in anger. I hate the Nazis for causing such pain to so many people. I don't want to be that skinny.

I moved to a different pile. It's there that I find a biography of a model. I read the reviews, her story seems interesting. The picture on the front cover looks healthy slim, no bones sticking out under her smooth skin. I stretched on Aunty Marta's bed and started to browse. She lures the reader to her uncensored world by slowly walking you through her life journey. From ordinary life to the extraordinary world that is fashion. Some of the pictures portray her skinny body. I don't want to become that skinny, but I am fascinated by her story so I took the book and now I have it under my pillow for my sweet night read.

05-01-2000

How funny, I couldn't put the book down after I opened it yesterday. I read pages upon pages. I love her life story and the pictures are so vivid. Some are taken at what looks like a private party. In the one I'm looking right now, she is drinking while dancing sandwiched between two sweaty muscled men. You can see her nipples through the silk pink dress, which looks like a nightdress. In another picture she is sitting on a toilet seat laughing with a white mark on her back hand. I swear I am never going to behave like that if I become skinny.

Okay. I love, love this chapter. She writes about her routine to stay thin. The list is long, but I want to write few things down so I remember:

When I started modelling that world was new to me. Although for half of my life I was tease because I was skinny, for most model agents I was not skinny enough. Some girls told me that to lose the extra weight they work out every day in the gym. The idea of working out daily at the gym drained me, because I must confess I am lazy, with the capital L. But I wanted to lose weight fast and I believed that going to the gym was not going to help me. That's the reason I became addicted to dieting pills and laxatives.

Few weeks after taking those pills I started to see

some result. Some of the models were so envious of my new thinness, because that got me lot of work. I didn't have the curvaceous and tall figure some late eighties and early nineties supermodels had. My body was a new trend in the fashion industry and many photographers loved that because I was able to fit into any box.

My agent was impressed about how popular I was becoming. I was booked as often as I was available. I enjoyed, especially when I started to get jobs abroad, in places like China, Japan and Russia, where being tiny was so cool. I love travelling to different continents. But with so much travelling, and without adult supervision, came partying and junk food binging. I was taking the laxatives and dieting pills throughout this period but after sometime the weight started to show around my butt. And a butt on an androgynous body model meant end of career. So I went to the old way of quick diet fix, purging. It was liberating when I managed to get rid of the meal. But with that something else started to happen to me, my beautiful white teeth started to stain. In my state of *madness*, what I was most interested in was my belly going down after each meal. I didn't think about the consequences. I would eat plate upon plate of delicious Chinese meals then excuse myself a few minutes later to go and get rid of everything. I would come back and order dessert without feeling guilt. People around me didn't get a clue of how I could eat all that food and stay so thin. I blamed it on a good gene pool. But if they really knew me, they would know that my mother was overweight and my father – well, he was never around to be seen.

This story is so inspiring. I look and look at the pictures. I know every detail. I know the type of pills she uses. The next chapter is all about how she develops anorexia. I am not interested in this chapter because I am never, EVER, going to become anorexic. I just want to be skinny and if using dieting pills will help me achieve my goal then that's welcome, but I swear, I am not going to let myself slim down as much as she did.

Right now I am worried about how to get the dieting pills. The only ones I can get my hands on without suspicion are laxatives. I am scared of purging, imagine my fingers scratching my throat. Thinking about all this makes me wanna weigh myself... STILL 57kg. AHHAHAHHHHH! I want to pull my hair! That sucks!!! How can I lose the extra kilo before Tuesday? I hate myself so much. Brad is right to call me fat! He is SO RIGHT. Why can't I lose weight easily as some girls do? Maybe purging can help. I came back from my very close encounter with the WC. I want to do it over and over again. I know I can do it, I won't scratch my throat. I feel light already.

06-01-2000

I want to DIE, if something doesn't happen to me by next week I will set the date to commit suicide, school was AWFUL! I feel AWFUL, awful.

This is how the day went.

In the morning I made the first mistake to weigh before drinking water as my breakfast. I weighed 57.5 kg, I feel ugly and fat. At school I couldn't bare looking at Brad. He was so awesome. But he flirted with some of the cheerleaders, especially Gianna. The other girls were laughing behind my back. I'm sure they are celebrating right now because Brad and I are not together anymore.

Carla was a bitch; she came over to me while I was talking to Ambra at break to ask, "Susanna, why aren't you eating?"

"I'm not hungry..." I don't know why she was interested.

"Well, maybe that's good for you, because you look a little chubby around the waist." I took it very bad and later I went to the toilet to cry. I cried over Carla's comment and Brad flirting with Gianna. Before the bell rang for the end of break I wet my face with cold water to cool down any redness.

Tonight I vomited after meal, I felt nauseous and the food was in my chest. I feel my worries overcoming me. After vomiting I felt good, but I swear I don't want to do it every time I eat. But Brad's eyes are like mirror. They reflect the memories with him. I can't get rid of them. I don't know how I'm going to survive the whole week with him sitting few seats away from me. He is not sitting behind me. Now he's sitting behind Melanie, she doesn't seem pleased with the new arrangement just like me.

How could he have been so nice to me for six whole weeks and just under two weeks treat me as if I never existed. Has he forgotten about our kisses, about his fingers running through my hair as if I was the only important human being on earth? My heart is thrown under a car. I want to hate him, but I rather die than hate him. I love him so much!

CHAPTER 34
Verona, Italy, July 2000

Trigger takes the limelight and talks the whole time at group therapy. As if she was new there, she starts by saying, "Hi everyone, I'm Veronica White but many of you know me as 'Trigger'. I moved to Verona about ten years ago from North America due to my father's work.

Back in Canada, I was a cheerleader. I have to admit, I liked my body but I felt the pressure to stay slim, so I started limiting my calories intake to 900 and slowly dropping it to 800. I made sure I ate only negative calorie food such as cucumber, celery, rice crackers and all kind of salad. I also cut down my carbohydrate, fast food, soda, deep fried food and sweets. I replaced them with lots of tofu, fish and fruit. When I felt like treating myself I binged then purged everything. I knew I was killing my liver, but really who cares when all I could see was the weight coming off so easily. And getting more compliments boosted my passion for seeking thinness; let's just say everything went a little bit far."

Veronica runs her fingers through her wavy hair, stretches her neck at the ceiling then continues, "Though I voluntarily decided to come into therapy because I love life more than I care about the numbers on the scale, when I came here I was worse than ever before." She smiles, shakes her head "I was such a diva, rude and tried every possible way to sabotage my therapy. I wouldn't talk... I'm so ashamed to admit it but once I even started smoking when I knew I shouldn't. But the voice inside was so strong and every word it said was a command."

"Where did you get the nickname Trigger?" one of the new girls asks.

"Oh, that nickname was given to me as soon as I walked through the main door. I was wearing a very revealing tank-top through which you could see my sagging bra, over a pair of short shorts. It was such bad fashion sense. Someone thought it was triggering. So the name stuck."

"How do you feel about yourself now?" the same girl asks

"I feel better. It's such a relief to not be scared to feel the meat around my waist. To not be afraid to eat without fighting or feeling like I need to burn the food off by torturing myself on a treadmill, or by doing crunches, push-ups… you name it. When I came here I was part ready and part not. Giving up control over my body was such a scary thing for me, but I wanted to get better so much. I wanted to have my period, eat and feel healthy. But most of all I wanted to enjoy who I am without feeling that to have a 'kickass' body, anorexia is my only option.

"Maybe the same guys who found me attractive might think I look like a monster with my new weight, but I feel good and I'm happy to be me. I feel more energetic and happy, but most of all my mind has found a new balance with how to view the girl in the mirror. I love when my family comes to visit and I don't feel like they are trying to take my happiness away by forcing me to eat." She looks at Susanna and winks.

"I know there is difference between my condition and some of you, but you have to understand we are the sick ones and not those who do not have anorexia. The funny thing is that when I was going through my bulimia, I thought everyone who was thin had anorexia, but that's not the case. You cannot compare yourself to another person because you end up dying while they live because they never had problem." She takes a deep breath.

"What do you see when you look in the mirror?" the coordinator asks her.

"A happy young woman, who doesn't wish to strangle the image staring back at her. In fact, I would like to hug her tight and say everything is okay." A tear escapes at the corner of her eye. "I really hope each one of you will come to accept yourself without feeling that losing weight and pretending to be someone else will make you happier. I know I was difficult when I came here initially, but I'm glad and grateful that the nurses and doctors were patient with me. I wish you all the best. Susanna?" Every eye in the room turn on Susanna who straights up. "Yep, you. Know that people truly love you and they care about your wellbeing."

Susanna looks at her fingernails, she keeps the tears at bay because she doesn't want to tear up in front of everyone. Her mind travels to her personal therapist. The images of her sitting there as a stone while he gives her advice on how to cope, deal and move forward from anorexia flicks on her mind reel. Until this group therapy, she has never taken his words on board, because she wasn't ready. At each appointment, he would patiently speak, while she sat there lost in her own thoughts. She would nod occasionally to make him think she was listening to him but all along his words would be water on oil to her ears. Listening to Veronica's words, she feels like there is a light at the end of the dark tunnel.

"I'm going to miss you so much." Susanna mumbles in Veronica's thick brown hair as she hugs her after the session.

"Me too, but get well soon so we can meet up outside this prison." Veronica smiles. She holds Susanna's shoulders and brings her face closer to Susanna's. "You are beautiful and you don't need ED or anyone to make you feel beautiful and special. Now, come help me pack. Tomorrow I'm free from the explosive farting of my roommate." She presses a kiss on Susanna's cheek.

That evening Susanna can't sleep. Her mental battle between needing help and wanting ED, as she has been calling it lately, is fierce. She understands that loving herself again depends on admitting she has an illness, *but who is easily ready to give up on something that gave such power?* Veronica's words echo in her ears, but Susanna is confused. *I want the demons of ED to help me fall deeper. I've been started viewing it as a personal coach. Every time I put the spoon in my mouth the nurse believes I am getting closer to my goal of 'ideal' weight, but they can't tell my mind to stop loving ED. I know that to get through this treatment I need to have a positive attitude, but ED doesn't want to hear about it.*

During the day, when I'm under supervision, I like to take the power from his hands. But at night, when everything is quiet and all I can hear are the giggles of the night nurses, I wrap my arms around him for dear life. He keeps me cosy with his negative attitude. During those midnight musings, I allow him to point out my biggest fear: looking like normal, getting to the point at which I will not be medically classifiable as anorexic. At that point I can be discharged even if mentally I would still be ED's lover. If I am ever discharged, what am I going to do? Who am I going to be like? I am scared of losing ED, but I am also scared of losing my life. I can't have them both. I have to give up on one of them.

She knows it's all in her mind. She concludes but another force wants her to gain her freedom and not lose this battle.

These thoughts are Susanna's midnight torturers, they crawl into her when she least expects. Tonight, instead of letting go of her wish to regain her freedom from ED, she opens her diary and begins to write.

Choosing between life and ED is the hardest thing I have to do.

As Dr. Gaetano said to be healthy it's a bit more than "admitting" – accepting the fact that I'm ill, being able to get the food down without the compulsive urge to purge or puke. Getting over feeling ill when I eat.

However, I know the first step would be admitting to the fact that my eating habits are all wrong, that I'm ill and I need help.

Yet, I feel like an elephant in deep water, light yet heavy. I am fighting to stay afloat. I am scared to open up. What if I fall again while facing the demons? I want to run away from the truth. As I've been told when it comes to an eating disorder, it is all about process. One cannot ever fully say they are recovered from ED. What I can do is to ~~talk~~ write about it, because I can't tell anyone how I really feel. Maybe writing my thoughts down will help me make sense of certain things.

Though no one is going to read my diary, I still find it hard to put down my thoughts, I feel so vulnerable. Writing feels like breaking up with my boyfriend and not telling him face to face. My throat is dry and my eyes are about to rain. ED is at the back of my mind telling me to close this diary because I need him and without him I am nothing. He might be right, I don't know where to begin. But I know I can't let ED win. It's written somewhere that if you are in a bad relationship you have to break free, but what I've never read is that it can be damn difficult to recognise you are in a bad relationship.

Natalie's letter is open in front of me. I cry every time I read Nat's son's name: Nathan.

Such a beautiful name, she wrote it means *God's gift*.

I think it's appropriate for him because he was a gift from God. I don't remember being such a believer before my "condition", but the way Nathan wasn't here just a few months ago shows how incredible life is.

I'm cross with myself. I can't believe I didn't know my friend was expecting all this time. At a time she needed me the most. And I wasn't there for her. Maybe, deep down, I suspected the reason she was putting on weight, but I didn't want to deal with any more stress. I was so wrapped up in my own world that I didn't see that she was growing a life in her womb.

I'm so sorry, but what makes me feel worse is how nice she is to want me to be Nathan's godmother. My heart is in my throat. She sent a picture of my godchild. (Yes, she's asked me to be his godmother!)

He is so cute. He has dark curls and a heart-shaped mouth. I don't know who he looks like just yet but I know I love him and I can't wait to hug him.

I feel the meaning in his name washing over me. God has given me this life and I don't want to waste it. I want to fight my illness for myself, for my family, for health, happiness and now Nathan, my cute godson.

I find it hard to let my therapist know the truth about my state of mind so maybe I can become my own therapist.

Question: Where are you right now?

Answer: I am sitting at my desk in my room at the Department of Psychology and Recovery, Verona General Hospital.

Q: Why are you here?

A: Because my parents decided that I need help to overcome ED.

Q: Good, you are making progress. Now tell me, when

did you come here?

A: I've lost count. It seems so long ago but the calendar tells me I first came here in March, then April.

Q: What happened? Why did you come here?

A: It's a long story. I don't want to bore you with it.

Q: Oh, I like stories, the longer the better. I don't have anything better to do, so tell me a story.

A: But I am so ashamed.

Q: Don't be.

A: Okay then. I might as well tell this story, because I am not the only one to have had the bad encounter with ED. My story doesn't stand out among the millions, also nobody will read this diary. I want to tell you how I got here.

ACKNOWLEDGEMENTS

To my children, Aaliyah and Tobias, *grazie*, you're my pride, my inspiration, my greatest achievement.

Thank you:
Maa, for raising me in beautiful Italy. Sally, for your passion for literature and art. Opoku, Oppong, and Gennaro; Cynthia, my big sister, for loving Brad and Susanna, for your invaluable encouragement throughout this writing journey. My writing companions, my one and only Writer's Group, for believing and sharing your beautiful writing with me; Lisa Baldiserra for reading first drafts, for remembering Italy together. Jennie E. Hunter, my beta-reader, for your insightful feedback.

My deepest thank you to all the writers that I've had the pleasure to work with through the Writers in Residence program at Saskatoon Library; your experiences and skills birthed this book. Yvette Nolan for telling me "Just write…"
David Paulsen for helping me put grit into the story and for introducing me to a great editor such as Sylvia McConnell. Rosemary Nixon for teaching me how killing my "darlings" will only enhance my story. Alice Kuipers, you're the first Writer in Residence that commented "I love Susanna already".

Last but certainly not least, thank you to my bloggy friends, your cheers are so appreciated. To you reader, thanks trillions for reading this novel, may you stay true to yourself.

THEODORA O. AGYEMAN-ANANE is writer and photographer, born Ghanaian and raised in Italy, she spent her formative years commuting from Vicenza to Verona, Italy, to study Optics but all she dreamt of was writing and photographing. She is living her dream in Saskatchewan, Canada, with her husband and two children. *Wasting Away* is her first novel.

Made in the USA
Charleston, SC
22 September 2015